Douglas Ainslie, Press Chiswick

Escarlamonde and other poems

Douglas Ainslie, Press Chiswick

Escarlamonde and other poems

ISBN/EAN: 9783744722919

Printed in Europe, USA, Canada, Australia, Japan

Cover: Foto ©Andreas Hilbeck / pixelio.de

More available books at **www.hansebooks.com**

ESCARLAMONDE

AND OTHER POEMS.

BY

DOUGLAS AINSLIE.

LONDON :

GEORGE BELL & SONS

AND NEW YORK.

1893.

TO

J. P. N.

AND TO THE MEMORY OF

S. G.

THIS BOOK IS

Dedicated.

CONTENTS.

	PAGE
ESCARLAMONDE	3
OFF THE HARBOUR OF MESSINA	73
THE LEGEND OF ST. AGNES	83
SONNET TO WORDSWORTH	91
TO SOME SUNFLOWERS	92
THE QUESTION	94
THE LUNATIC	95
SONNET ON "THE SORCERESS," PORTRAIT BY GRAHAM ROBERTSON	96
MNEMOSYNE	97
A SONNET OF POISONS	99
THE DREAM	100
A BALLAD OF BIRDS	101
THE GALLERY	103
TO A MARBLE MASTERPIECE	104
DHU VORN	105
SYMBOLISM	106
THE FURNACE	107
THE VISION	108

	PAGE
SPRINGTIME	109
MEMORY	110
MUSIC	112
THE DEATH OF ARETINO	113
THE VISION	121
HYMN	127
THE SPHINX	128
AFTER READING MAETERLINCK'S "AVEUGLES"	129
SARAH BERNHARDT AS THEODORA ENTHRONED	130
WITH A COPY OF KEATS	131
"BLUE-RAVEN LOCKS AND UNDER"	132
"'LET DOWN YOUR HAIR, SWEET SYBIL,' WAS MY PRAYER"	133
"HOW WISELY THE HEROES OF GREECE"	134
LOVE (A CONCEIT)	135
INTERJECTIONS	136
A POETIC CREED REVERSED	138
POSTSCRIPT	139

ESCARLAMONDE.

CARMINIS PERSONÆ.

COUNT OF TOULOUSE (*Raymond*).
COUNT OF FOIX (*Roger*).
COUNT OF COMMINGES. } *Albigensians.*
COUNT OF BÉZIERS.
COUNT SIMON DE MONTFORT. } *Crusading*
COUNT GUY DE MONTFORT (*His son*). } *Barons.*
PIERRE DE CASTELNAU. } *Papal Legates.*
THÉDISE.
ROLAND (*The Troubadour*).
GREEN GREGORY.

ALIX (*Countess of Toulouse*).
ESCARLAMONDE (*Her daughter*).

Other Barons on both sides, Knights, Attendants,
Jongleur.

PLACE.—*Toulouse and Crusaders' camp twenty miles off.*

TIME.— 1208.

ESCARLAMONDE.

ACT I.

SCENE I.—*Toulouse.* RAYMOND'S *Court.*

COUNT RAYMOND *and his* Barons, ALIX *and*
ESCARLAMONDE, Attendants.

Toulouse. (*Addressing* FOIX, BÉZIERS *and*
COMMINGES.)

MY Lords of Béziers, Comminges and Foix,
I summoned you upon this ninth of June,
That with my chiefest vassals I should meet
Pierre, Legate of his mighty Holiness,
Pope Innocent the Third, and Guy de Montfort,
His colleague, envoy of the temporal powers.
And why that woman state, the Papal See,
Has wedded the great swords of northern France
Burgundy, Montfort, Bar, Nevers, which point
Unsheathed against my breast, it will be well
Ere the ambassadors are introduced,
That in a few clear words I set before you.

Albeit the causes of this armament
May seem as strange as any fairy tale
Yet are they true, but like the fairy tale
Have their hid moral, which who runs may
        read ;—
" Qui hait son chien lui met la rage sus."
This Pierre de Castelnau is not the first
By many of the Rome-born, raven crew,
That cross the Alps to croak of sacrilege.
One out of many instances will show
Their evil will ; two years ago, they said,
While Abbot Plantin preached one day, that I
Did urge my yonder fool, green Gregory,
To mimic the divine and did lie back
Loud laughing in my stall ;—only half true,
For Gregory began without command
To make wry faces, as divinely quaint
As Plantin's were divine, but the next day
He was well beaten ; were you not, sirrah ?

 Gregory. Zebraed, most noble Raymond.

 Toulouse.   None the less,
From Rome came notice, that on all my lands
Lay ban and interdict, and would so lie
Till penance had been done. I went to Rome
And kneeling to his Holiness the Pope
Explained how this had come about, that I

Who loved God well, loved hawking near as
    much
And was more prone to take the hawk at Puys [1]
Than spend the summer saying orisons.
Innocent smiled, and turning to Thédise,
Said, " Surely here we have no heretic :
Count Raymond loves 'parage ;'[2] nor is at
    enmity
With our most Holy Church ;" and therewithal
Granted me absolution and rare gifts ;—
St. Peter's tooth and a cornelian ring
Carved with his name, " Pope Innocent the
    Third."
I promised, ere I left the Papal Court,
To aid the legates in abolishing
All heresy from my estates ; and here
Lay the sunk rock on which our peace has
    split.

[1] *To take the hawk at Puys.*—The knight who took
the hawk from the perch where it was exhibited at Puys,
thereby pledged himself to provide amusements for his
companions throughout the coming year.

[2] *Parage.*—This word means *nobility* of all kinds, and
is used by transference for its appanages.

    " Her name was Berengere, fair woman of age,
    Was ther non hir Pere of no heiere parage."
                  LANGTOFT, *Chron.*

For soon I found that easier it were
To gather up Toulouse and set her down
Elsewhere, an exile to herself, than drive
All "heretics" away, for all were heretics,
Or, if not all, those that obeyed the Pope
Were heretics, so vastly larger pressed
The multitude of Albigensians.
What can a prince's will, howe'er revered,
Prevail against his peoples' counter-faith?
This I explained to Foulques, our bishop here
Whose horses could not water for the mob
That aye went crying " Popery, avaunt!"
And drove the poor beasts back. But Thédise saw
In all the insurrection my one hand
Stirring the stormy sea; he therefore laid
Afresh the interdict, and this man Pierre,
This Pierre de Castelnau is of that breed:
He will no whit forgive, no whit forget,
His life is naught but hate for love of God.
The embassy that now awaits my will
Bears the conditions of the Roman Church.
Therefore, brave Foix, Comminges, and Béziers
I pray you say whether, in case the peace
Cost dearer than endurance, you will fight
For me or Montfort;—there's no golden mean.
First, let Comminges, my senior vassal, speak.

Comminges. Most noble Count, with sorrow
    and alarm,
I see you near the cataract of war.
I am old now, so old that my advice
May taste of dotage, but for what it's worth
I give it with a prayer for all our souls.
Receive the Legates well, and to their terms,
Whate'er they be, make no hasty dissent :
Remember that against the combined force
Of France and Germany we have but gained
Your cousin, King of Aragon, and stand
Outnumbered six to one.   I say no more,
Save that for me and mine we're always yours,
And will fight for you to our last blood-drop.
    Toulouse. Sincerest thanks, most faithful
    friend, Comminges.
    Foix. For me, my lord, yours is the only
    side,
From inclination and necessity.
Twice have I met the Holy Roman Church ;
Twice have we parted, scarce the best of friends.
Our first encounter was a half-year back
Outside my town of Foix ; the priests were
    bearing
The bones of some dead saint in a procession ;
I passed them, mounted, laughing, and my head,

In their own words, showed "lofty as a stag's :"
Whereon this Legate dog and fellow curs
Followed my horse's heels and dared to lay
The curses of the Church upon my soul.
Hearing them curse me and to clearly show
How much I feared them or their woman's creed,
I bad turn bridle that we all might seek
The nearest church ; my knaves threw wide the
   doors
And on my jennet, Rosy Queen, I rode
Up to the altar, where we foddered her,
Mixing the wine with water for her thirst.
Again, three months ago came Gaston Bois
Bearing a tale of how the scorpion priests
Had stung his mother with their tongues and
   driven
The lady forth from Pamiers, I but rode
Across to Pamiers and laid low the head
Of a black raven, croaking out his mass ;
The monks and abbot, well-nigh dead with fear,
Offered me absolution for their lives :
But above all these things and if I were
Most virtuous Catholic in the whole Provence,
Yonder fair lady, bright Escarlamonde,
Your sister and my long-affianced bride,
Would magnetize the mountain of my faith

And draw me back to her sweet heresy.
Therefore, most noble Count, receive my sword,
Hers is my heart.

    Toulouse.   Best thanks, my noble Bertram ;
These troubles over, mine the care shall be
To graft her rosebud on your standard tree.

    Béziers. Last year the Legate travelled Béziers
        through,
" To drive lambs back to fold," and sought from
        me
Homage to Rome ; he whispered in my ear,
" If you will now abjure your vassaldom
To the Count Raymond and be ours, you're
        saved ;
If not, that very hand whereon you lean,
A sorry prop, shall hurl you in the dust."
" Words dark as these," I answered, " may breed
        acts
Too dark for words, nevertheless, sir priest,
I love and fear you not, so go your ways,
Seek Rome again, say masses for my soul."
'Twas thus I made of choice necessity.

    Toulouse. Then I may count a trinity of
        friends,
Forming an unity of friendship ; thus
Bucklered about by such stout champions I

Dare Europe to pick up my fallen glove.
(*To a marshal.*) Let the ambassadors be ushered
    in.

    Enter GUY DE MONTFORT, PIERRE DE
        CASTELNAU, *Papal Legate, with*
        Attendants.

    Toulouse. Pierre, Papal Legate, Guy de Mont-
      fort, you,
Son and ambassador of Simon Montfort,
The Earl of Leicester, general in chief
Of the invading army, greeting, speak.
    Pierre. To you, Count Raymond, sixth Lord
      of Toulouse,
Duke of Narbonne and Marquis of Provence,
I bear these terms, concluded on at Arles,
By Thédise, Arnauld and the other priests
In mission from the Pope ; to them are joined
Eudes, the Duke of Burgundy, Simon Montfort,
Counts of Nevers, St. Pierre, Auxerre, Genève,
Trèves and a host of others, with their men,
Twenty-four thousand strong : the King of
      France, .
Philip, has hearkened to the Pope's appeal ;
And if to these conditions you are deaf,
Body and spirit, Church and State as one,

Blessed by the Lord and by his Holiness,
Shall burn with fire and utterly consume
The filthy foxes that destroy the vines.

Toulouse. (*Half aloud, and heard by* ROLAND
THE TROUBADOUR, *who stands just
behind him.*)

Who'll choke for me this croaking spawn of Paul?
(*Aloud.*) Have a care, master Legate ;
Anger me not too far, lest the sharp words
Now sheathed within my throat leap forth as
swords
And cleave your shaven pate. Put forth the
terms.

Pierre. (*Unrolling a manuscript which he
holds in his hand. Reads.*)

Count Raymond to disband his present army,
Dismiss his vassals, raze his castles level
With the flat plain, in all things to obey
And bow before the Church, to straightway drive
All heretics away from all the lands
Lying beneath his sway, that of his Court
Not one remain within Toulouse but all
Live rustic lives apart ; for glittering cloaks,
Bright caps and jewels, sombre hues alone,
And unadorned to serve, and of cooked meat
But two sorts to be ate in all the land.

When all these terms shall duly be fulfilled
Count Raymond is to join the knightly order
Known as Saint John's, and fight against the
      Turk :
Nor shall he ever seek his natal shores
Until the Legate grant him fullest grace.
If all these things be done, and it seem good
To the Count Montfort and the Legate, they
May pass Count Raymond back his lands again.
    Toulouse. If these be terms then peace is
      slavery ;
Through their black drapery of gall I see
The souls of those who planned them like a flock
Of vampire bats, which suck away men's lives
Between two dreams, but here 'tis morning still.
Avaunt ! Depart ! get thee back to the tomb,
Thou man of death, come from the land of death
That was the land of life ; tell Simon Montfort
That I will not myself strip off my flesh
To lie within the hollow of his grave ;
And ere thy vultures make me skeleton,
Who now am body and blood, they'll have to peck
Through many a mailèd coat, so it may chance
They break both beak and claws before the end.

---

[1] This is a translation from the original Latin.

Pierre. Is this the answer I am to report?

Toulouse. Yes, in the bowing of the summer
    corn
That yellows now through all my fair Provence;
Yes, in the rustle of the tuneful trees
Stooping to kiss their courtier gale of June;
In the quick sparkle of the distant stars;
In the immense gold glory of the sun;
In all my land and all my lieges see
One large defiance of the Papacy.   [*Rising.*
No stranger, friend or enemy, e'er went
Unfeasted from Toulouse, therefore I pray you
Follow me now to the great banquet-hall.

      [*Exeunt all but* R. DE TRENCAVEL.

Roland. "Who'll slay me yonder spawn of
    Paul?"
Thus spake Count Raymond, and methought his
    glance
Flashed under on my sword, for well he knew
None other dared the deed.   I will persuade
My jongleur, Jacques, to don the penitent's garb
And as the chosen representative
Of Castres, that once o'erteemed with heretics
But now seeks Papal grace, he shall implore
The presence of the Legate in his town.
Priests travel singly and I will await

His Eminence in the dark fir-tree wood
A league without Toulouse and thereby save
His Eminence all earthly journeys more.
Then come the worst I shall have done my
      best
For love of Raymond and Escarlamonde—
Escarlamonde for whom the Creator needed
So many colours, such pure chosen white,
Such roses, such large pearls, such golden
      showers,
Borrowed from earth, from heaven and crimson
      hell,
That ever working for ten thousand years
But now in this the latest point of time
He has produced the equal of himself,
And that the whole wide world should worship
      her
Has sent her for a moment in the skies
Robed in blue and called Escarlamonde.
I love her, fountain of all loveliness,
That flows in our Provence, there is a chain
By which all flowers, all birds, all music notes
Are bound to her gold girdle, every rose
That drops a petal doth one instant tinge
With pallor her fair cheeks and every bud
Springing to blossom re-illumines them

With palest blushes of a new-born pink,
So quickly doth her colour come and go.

Enter ESCARLAMONDE.

Escarlamonde. Roland, are we alone, I have
    but left
The banquet, seeking you?
    Roland.   My lovely one,
But shortly mine no longer.
    Escarlamonde.   Wherefore so,
Dear Roland?
    Roland. Heard you not Count Raymond's
    words
Of promise to the Count of Foix?
    Escarlamonde.   Such words
As you well know are only snares with him
To gain the Count of Foix, a waverer,
Toward the Crusaders' side and but restrained
By my betrothal; once the peace confirmed
(For Raymond loves him not) I will contrive
The severance, never fear, and then, dear
    Roland,
Your single name shall speak our double bliss.
            [*A voice calls* ESCARLAMONDE.
Yes, mother, now farewell, my dearest one.
              [*Exit* ESCARLAMONDE.

Enter GUY DE MONTFORT.

Guy. Roland de Trencavel, a word apart—
I sought you here.

‡ *Roland.* Say on then, Guy de Montfort ;
We are old friends, and I can ne'er forget
How once in Paris, taunted by a crew
Of vulgar roysterers as foreigner,
My circling sword had certain flashed no more
But for your sinewy aid ; I promised then
A fair return, and Roland's promises
Live with his life, not die upon his lips ;
Therefore if now I can by any means
Make deeds of words and help you to your ends
Speak them but forth.

Guy.   Roland, you have divined
Rightly, I sought you here with a request,
But not of life and death ; indeed I fear
Your laughter more than your assent, although
God knows for me 'tis more than life or death.

　　Roland. You love, Count Guy, or use a lover's
　　　　tongue ;
I ne'er had classed you with that piercèd band.

　　Guy. An hour agone I was love-free indeed.

　　Roland. Then that I may with every nerve
　　　　assist

In siege of love and loving stratagem
Tell me her name, her home is in Toulouse.

   Guy. In your hand lies the hope of all my life,
My peace in death, I love Escarlamonde.

   Roland. (*Aside.*) Why to the world is beauty
      beautiful ?   •

   Guy. For among all the fair and all the proud,
All the gold-garmented and golden-haired
Provençal ladies, to my sceptic eye
Always there lacked the crowning element—
That cross of beauty which on women shines
As on a church, to mark a holy place,
With them was golden, silver or mean brass,
But with Escarlamonde is diamond,
One burning jewel of most perfect form
That from the moment mine eyes lit on her
Darted its blinding radiance through my soul.
In your hand lies the joy of all my life,
My peace in death, I love Escarlamonde.

   Roland. Count Guy speaks as a poet out of place
Courting the countess of some foreign tower.

   Guy. I am no poet, fighting is my trade,
But stung by love till I could tear my heart
Out from my bosom for her smooth white teeth.

   Roland (*Smiling.*) Guillaume de Cabstaing's
      heart against his will

C

Was served to Countess Roussillon, if you
Would carve yours out for her, 'twill be my pleasure
To bear it to the fair Escarlamonde.

    Guy. Torture me not, but hearken to my
        prayer;
It is your blessed fate to wander free
In this bright town where even the pebble-stones
Along her garden walk have every day,
The glory to be crushed by her slight feet.
Your idlest seconds as you saunter here
In converse with the Queen Escarlamonde
Would, were they mine, weigh down eternity.

    Roland. Say on, what would you of me?

    Guy. I who was stranger, now am enemy,
And wretched lover shall ne'er see the walls
That prison all I love, until the peace.

    Roland. Methinks that those who seek the
        dove of peace
Should rather cast their searching glances back
To some dim island anchored in the past,
Where still the white bird coos and all-forgotten
White breast to breast the last true lovers cling.

    Guy. Too true, alas, too sadly true, and thence
Flows my request.

    Roland.   So far as with me lies
Fulfilment, you may trust my plighted word.

Guy. If you will bear Escarlamonde from me
Letters, and be the mirror of my love
Until the peace, when I may dare to woo,
Then is your ancient debt of friendship paid
A many times.

    Roland.   Such letters I will bear
And be the echo of your absent love.

    Guy. Ten thousand thanks most noble friend,
        Roland,
Best of brave friends, how glorious you look !

    Roland. Thank not too hastefully ; you saw
        just now
The Count of Foix.

    Guy.   One of Count Raymond's lords ?

    Roland. Escarlamonde is promised him for
        bride
When but the peace be signed.

    Guy.   I marked the Count ;
There sat he glowering on all around,
And when his gaze did fall upon his love
Grew dark instead of brighter, as the shade
Cast by grim tower when the sun outshines.
She cannot love him and the chance of war
Sows all anew the seed of destiny.
But say, dear Roland, is the Count of Foix
My only rival ?   . . .

Roland.   Yes, although there was
Another once did love her well, I think,
But he is dead or gone beyond the seas—
And yet I think he loved her very well.

Guy. So, good, I fear not Foix, and by your aid
Shall woo and win the fair Escarlamonde ;
And should de Montfort's son in aught avail
To smooth life's path for Roland, here he lays
His utmost stretch of power at Roland's feet,
By letters to the King of France or grants
Of lands and coin or the like help in love.

Roland. I must away ; adieu, I'll meet you in
        the hall :
Have ready the letter.

Enter Attendant.

Attendant. Count Raymond asks your presence
        in the hall
To quaff with him a parting stoup of wine.
        [*Exit* GUY DE MONTFORT *and* Attendant.

Enter JACQUES.

What think you ?

Roland. We have not time to think, but only
        act.

The Legate. . . .   [*Exeunt.*

SCENE II.—*A wood through which runs a path-
way.* ROLAND *discovered walking up and
down.*

Roland. I gave Jacques fullest orders, saw him
dressed
In cinders, girdled with a knotty scourge
As penitent from Castres who doth request
Humbly the absolution and the presence
Of the most holy Legate in his town,
Craving for pardon ; and the priestly law
Is to be everywhere the spirit calls.
And Jacques, my jongleur, clever, twinkling
Jacques,
The "penitent." Ha ! ha ! most holy Church
Ne'er bred the peacock in that jackdaw's skin ;
He will not fail. But hark ! i' the distance steps :
I must retreat lest yonder be not Pierre.
                    [*Disappears in the wood.*

Enter PIERRE.
Pierre. Narrow the way that leads to Paradise,
But I will wear the crown ; these men of Castres
Are sudden turned to God.

Enter ROLAND.

Roland. Salve ! Sir Priest.

Pierre. Salve ! Sir Knight. How many miles
    to Castres ?

Roland. Some six or seven, but prithee stay
    awhile
I would with you discourse theology.

Pierre. I cannot stay ; God's service calls me
    hence ;
I am the Legate Pierre.

Roland. (*Placing himself so as to intercept the
    Legate*).   My reverend father,
Haste ill becomes old age, and you shall stay
Till all be answered that my fancy craves.

Pierre. Loose me, base knight ; you are impor-
    tunate,
Full of vain words as are the heretics ;
And now, methinks, that I have seen your face
At Raymond's court ; you are a Troubadour,
One of those coloured marsh-flies that do haunt
Where most corruption reigns.

Roland.   If that were so
Then should I buzz about St. Peter's dome
And whisper in the scarlet harlot's ear
Tales of her own true sons, the cardinals,
Who worship Mary—but the Magdalene—

And quaff such seas of wine—the blood of
    Christ !—
That antique Bacchus, sleeping in the hill,
Waits but his tigers to be God again.

    Pierre. Fearful blasphemer, fall upon your
      knees
And pray for mercy, 'tis to purge Provence
Of such as you I come ; if yet there live
One lamb of God in all this fold of wolves
He may be saved alive.

    Roland. Enough ! you have your Gods and I
      have mine,
Poets did sing and make the only prayers
To strong, bright, golden, ever-verdant gods
Long ere the priests were born. An ugly God
Loves ugliness and therefore you exist.

    Pierre. To the infernal glow of hell's red blaze
There lacks the torment that will chasten you.
I *will* upon my way ; aside ! (*Striving*) give
    place !

    Roland. (*Thrusting him back.*) Black angel,
      bent upon your search for souls,
Know that in Castres, although I let you pass,
Dwells not an enemy to brave Count Raymond—
Raymond that means *parage* and chivalry—
I wrote the letter begging your attendance.

Pierre. Then will I to the camp.

Roland. No, not so fast.

[*Showing the swords.*

There hang two deaths above us in the air ;
These swords may cut both down, but one they
    will.

[*Offers one sword to* PIERRE, *who rejects it,
the weapon falls by his side.*

Pierre. (*Starting back.*) Those who take the
    sword
Shall by the sword be slain.

Roland. Then must you perish ;
Aye, had you twenty thousand lives, should perish
Justly as many times ; yes, your black robes,
Those soft hands hanging as though made to
    bless,
That smile where oil and honey seem to meet ;
All, all the swords unsheathed in Provence
They have discabbarded ; if all were slain
Who took the sword, then Rome were execution—
Blood flowing from the topmost Papal throne
(Where now rules Antichrist, Pope Innocent)
Over the whole world, plunged in bloody ruin
But by Rome's mitred art, her closet lore,
Her deaf ambition that doth ever lean
On ghostly fear and stalk about the world

Garnering power with promises of heaven,
Or smolting it with metaphors of hell.

[Offers the other sword.

Here are two swords, I say, choose which you
    will—
No choice is choice of death.

  Pierre. (*Crossing his arms and himself.*) I
    choose salvation.

  Roland. Then I prick forth your soul to join
    the saints.   [*Stabs him.*

  Pierre. (*Staggering. Then falls with clasped
    hands. In a faint voice, slowly.*)
I hear the angels flying,
Those large white wings on which they come to
    bear me
Rustle so distant soft to my faint sense.

    *   *   *   *   *

    *   *   *   *   *

[Gasping.

Mine too the martyr's crown, O thorn-crowned
    Christ !

    *   *   *   *   *

Mine as thy pardon to thy murderers.

    *   *   *   *   *

[Dies.

SCENE III.—*Toulouse. Afternoon of the fol-
lowing day. Outside* RAYMOND'S *palace.
A tree-shaded walk.* COMTE DE FOIX
and ESCARLAMONDE *discovered strolling
up and down.*

 Foix. I watched his eyes and all the while that
   Pierre
Read out the treaty or Count Raymond spoke
They centred on your face ; it is an insult
To my betrothed and one I should chastise
Were he of ours ; but you, I think, returned
With eager gaze his gazing.
 Escarlamonde.   You mistake,
Dear Roger, if Count Guy de Montfort's looks
Were fixed on me I could not therefore vanish :
In truth I saw him not, and had I seen
What could the face of a mere stranger knight
(And one, they say, to France an alien,
For though his father be the Poitiers count
Yet is he English and an enemy)
Work upon me who am your promised bride ?
 Foix. Indeed I know not, save that women's
   wills
Outvie the winds that laugh at compasses ;—

For what can Montfort give a bride as I
Who next your brother am the richest baron
In all the southern France, my stables full
Of fiery chargers that do stamp and shake
The burnished armour hanging in my hall?
Beneath my banner gather clouds of strength —
Great brawny loons whose blows breed victory.
My coffers teem with gold and I have jewels
To buy a queen to wife, but I will you,
My gentle soft, my fair Escarlamonde !

    [*Draws her to him and kisses her. She
      returns his kiss.*

    Escarlamonde. There, there, you kiss me like
      a husband, Roger ;
And we're not married yet ;—lo, yonder, Roland
The Troubadour who cometh this way, strolling ;
He rarely wanders from the land of dreams,
But when he does there ever seem to glisten
On his pale forehead pearls of fairyland.

    Foix. Another of your swains and one less
      worthy
Than even Guy de Montfort.   Roland's father
(A solitary watcher of the sea,
Who's long since dead) had but one lonely tower :
His son, you know, has sold it and doth cater
In tunes your brother's favour ; that his race

Is old with oldest no man will deny
But sunk below the wasting of your smile ;
And I—have all.

    Escarlamonde. (*Aside.*) Yes, you have all ; his
      nothing 'tis I love.

Enter ROLAND. *Bows to* ESCARLAMONDE
        and FOIX.

    Foix. Good morrow, Troubadour, you bring us
      songs,
Or such-like toys?

    Roland.   Did you not say just now
"All things are mine"? permit me to salute
The "Lord of everything" who cannot want
For worthless rhyming ware.

    Escarlamonde.   Ah ! Roland, peace !
You and the Count are friends.

    Foix.   Ay, friends indeed—
Methinks, de Trencavel, your wit were wont
Be sharper once than now, prithee beware
It rust not and you straightway lose your place.

    Roland. The noble Count says true ; I've lately
      lacked
Of something dull whereon to edge my wit ;
But the high honour of his company
Serves well the turn ; I do again salute

The Count of Foix.

Foix.   I and the Countess here
Discoursed of private matters.

Roland.   If the Countess
Ask for my absence, I am like the wind,
Here, the next moment gone.

Escarlamonde.   Why are you both
So fiery foolish? Greet and be good friends.

Foix. I see then that you seek his company.
Farewell: de Trencavel, we meet again. [*Exit.*

Escarlamonde. Thus high-intolerant is the
        Count of Foix,
He holds himself the one knight paragon,
The star of maidens' eyes. How long it is
Since I have seen de Trencavel pass by !

Roland. And now I come, but bearer of a
        letter
From a dear friend.

Escarlamonde. (*Laughing.*) Who, may I ask,
        is he?

Roland. He is a soul to whom all earthly
        things
Did float in a pale mist, so that he saw
But shades for men, and as for women shades
Of shadows, so was all his life a mist ;
Till suddenly at midday through those clouds

Shot the bright ray of more than earthly light
Which to most mortals is Escarlamonde,
To some the sun—

    Escarlamonde.   His name, his name, I pray.

    Roland. In letters making up such words as
        "Truth,"
"Virtue and Chivalry," or "Continence,"
"Steadfast in Aim," "Firm Friend," "Fierce
        Enemy,"
"Love till the Death," there sleeps the very
        echo
Aye follows on his name, but to your ears
It may sound harshly.

    Escarlamonde.   Prithee, sweet Roland,
Spare me more waiting, I must hear it now.

    Roland. I pray you be not frighted at the name,
He loves you well that bears it, as will show
The letter.

    Escarlamonde. How strange you are, dear
        Roland, swiftly wrought
From poet-chivalrous to messenger
Of love to me your love ; those airy gods
Who do but brush *our* cheeks with windy wings
Or kiss them in the rain, I think to poets
Whisper the secrets of the universe,
Half raise for them the veil so that they wander

Awry and stumbling through the world and
    follow
Some more than earthly phantom of the fair
Whereof they throw the shadow in their songs,
And then die young with large, sad, seeking eyes.
I have always
Loved poets more than kings—a monarch's lips
Are but the trumpet sounding to his people
Words of command—the king is but a man
Imperial for life ; his memory buried
By the next king, imperial as he,
But a true poet bears upon his lips
Deep organ notes that when his voice is hushed
Still cling about the aisles of all the world,
As sweet as in his early summer day
Spent sonnet-wreathing with each stop a kiss.
(*Pauses.*) I promise all you ask, but some new
    fancy,
This time, dear Roland, leads you far afield.
What is his name?

    Roland.   Count Guy de Montfort.

    Escarlamonde. Young Count Montfort,
Who gazed so wistful-sadly standing there,
Gold-plumed, black-armoured heavy-helmeted,
So tired-souled, so blind of aspiration,
I thought him of the bruised, storm-beaten band

Whose eyes look backward when they seek their
    love.

Roland. No, he was born a seeker of the sun,
Far off in England, and his father's court,
Where flowers sought a license when to bloom,
Froze his whole soul, so that he thanks these
    wars
Have borne him hitherward where men may
    catch
One ray of light before their evening comes.
Here is the letter.

Escarlamonde. (*Reads.*) My salvation or my
sepulchre, my eagle or my dove, my essence
of all sweet epithets, or incarnation of all that
burns. These wild, hasty words *may* reach you.
I have loved you since first I saw you—two
hours ago—I will not add forever—foolish word
that knows not how many centuries lie for lovers
in a second. My best friend, Roland, bears this
paper. Send by him a promise of friendship
till the war has end, then of fairness in your
choice between De Foix and Guy de Montfort,
or send me nothing—which is death.

GUY DE MONTFORT.

Roland. There lies true love, or love was never
    true.

Escarlamonde. But I have never spoken to
    Count Guy :
What can I answer to this moon-struck knight ?
  Roland. Answer him merely : " Keep your
    life, my friend :
Await and watch : no promise either way :
Time breeds all marvels : let us trust to time."
  Escarlamonde. Well, dear knight Roland,
    then I write your words ;
For you, your words, dear Roland, and return
As soon as written : wait me one moment here.
                                  [*Exit.*
  Roland. So I have sold my peace to Guy de
    Montfort.
She shines more steady radiant this pale night
Than cruellest star to watcher upon earth.
  Escarlamonde. (*Re-entering.*) Here is the
    letter ; I have told him shortly
That ere the war be ended, my dear brother
Will not allow me marry Roger Foix,
Therefore to cease despair. (*Aside.*) Ah ! Roland,
    darling,
What crimes for love against love's self I do !
  Roland. Then to the camp this evening, under
    night
I should be safe.

                D

Escarlamonde.　But you will bear the answer,
And talk with me a little of Count Guy,
Or even drop some honey from your lips,
Gathered where bees sip from a vocal flower?
　　Roland. Adieu, I come again ; the wings of
　　　friendship
Will bear me there and back ;
Adieu, adieu !　　　　　　　　　　[*Exit* ROLAND.

Enter ALIX.

　　Alix. Where is the Count of Foix ; I left him
　　　with you
Not half an hour agone?　He is the husband
You need to curb that wild, unruly spirit :
Would God the wars were over !　Roland there
Is dangerous—as every troubadour ;
He must no more alone with you consort.
　　Escarlamonde. Count Foix was with me, but
　　　when Roland came
Departed, like a cloud before the sun,
Albeit I bade him tarry, no, he went,
Proud beyond praises, puffed to bursting power
By his own emptiness, filled full of wealth.
But for my Roland, the good Troubadour,
As brave a knight as any that can carve
But flesh with swords, while he with heron's plume

Blazons his scutcheon on eternity,
I rarely see him, though whene'er he brightens
My garden with his smile, the little pansies,
Those floral butterflies, ope wide their wings
And say, "Ah joy! a brother comes to us;"
The rose stoops forward, blushing to her stem,
And sighs, "Ah! pluck me from oblivion;"
All, all the vernal blooms, all summer glories
Bend smiling toward him; least of all am I,
But with the modest violets I stand
Gazing upon him with our bluest eyes;
He bows and passes, humming some half-tune,
Some lyric anthem, clarioned in heaven,
On earth a whisper even to poet's ears;—
I will not drive my Troubadour away.

    Alix. Perchance your ears are closèd to the
        rumours
That rise through all the town; the day when
        Pierre
Was foully murdered by an unknown knave,
Roland de Trencaval, in muffling cloak,
With hasty steps was seen to quit Toulouse
On the same road by which within the hour
The legate left for Castres,—there's little doubt
His was the sword that slew the man of God.
If this be true, to every honest soul,

Though justice fail to seize his guilty body,
The name of Roland must swing gallows high.
　　Escarlamonde. I answer first that many men
　　　　have travelled
To Castres and slain no legate on the way,
And so may Roland ;—but I grant the murder,
My dearest mother, merely to declare
How slight a thing I hold an ugly life ;
When on my glistening gravel-path there crawls
A slimy snail, I call a gardener lad
To crush it with his heel : far more my brother,
When over all his lands a reptile writhes
Distilling papal poison, rightly seeks
His truest friend to rid him of the beast.
But I say further ; yea, if Roland's sword,
Bright as the sun, clear flashing as his eye,
Had plunged the point of death in half the hearts
That beat in vulgar bosoms through Provence ;
If in Toulouse he wrought a crime undreamed
On earth, that were a bane to fieriest hell,
Yet were he Roland and his arms my heaven.
　　Alix. I am a traveller from seventy years :
How swiftly all things change !—such words as
　　　　these
Strike foreign on my hearing.　When I married
Your father, the fifth Raymond, none but bowed

His knee before the Pope ; how wild soe'er
His life had been, he feared the Holy Church.
Now there seems wine got into daily life
Leaving no reverence, no reticence,
None of the pure, unspoken, maiden love,
None of the lofty, humble chivalry.
Each one will glow, be he a very sun,
Like yonder Roland, of iniquity,
Or a mere worm with stolen hedge-row light.
How mad is now the world ! To me there
      comes
From all these feasts and frolics but one sense ;
All nature seems to say, "Adieu, farewell,"
Your day is lived, seek the long-open grave ;
But ere I go, one duty calls on me,—
Your brother must beware the Troubadour.
    Escarlamonde. Ah, mother, mother dearest,
      spare me that ;
My brother loveth Roland, and your words
Would make him hate me, never love him less ;
Besides, though I love Roland, well I know,
That Foix has bought me with his armèd men,
His horses, his great name in war, his riches ;
I must be his, therefore pray, mother, pray,
I pray you leave this web unweave itself.
You fear, not hate our life, for you are old,

And always in the present you discern
Your youth disformed ; for me these modern
    deeds,
Which make the world quake, grew up with my
    birth.
I am twin sister of the new-born life,
And therefore love. it sisterly ; I feel
Through all the air throb some strange vital scent
That seems to spring from Roland, for whene'er
His eyes meet mine they centre all my thoughts ;
He loves me not, or but as a bright bird
Among bright birds new-lit upon the tree
Where he sings loudest, king of nightingales.
No priest, no wedding-ring, nor marriage-vow
Can ever kill the Roland in my soul.
And come what may, though all the furies turn
On one poor maid, I love him utterly.
    Alix.   Maddest maid,
My feeble hand shall save you from yourself
And this mad time ; I'll to your brother straight.
                                        [*Exit.*

    Escarlamonde. Ah ! stony-hearted mother of
    my tears,
Mere name of mother, well I know your will
Is iron to entreaty, but my Raymond,
Like a clear river flowing toward the sea,

Glides laughing over lesser obstacles,
Submerging rocks that dare to stem his stream ;
Therefore he will but smile at mother's tale,
And love that fears light laughter is not love :
I'll laugh their laughter back and turn to tune
The discord of the whole court's raillery.

[*Exit.*

END OF ACT I.

ACT II.

SCENE I.

Toulouse. (*Pointing upward.*) Yonder, me
    thinks, the highest of the three,
Hanging aloft, like beauty-spots in heaven,
Is my brave tiercel Jean.
   Falconer.   'Tis so, my lord.
   Toulouse.   (*Taking several rapid steps
    forward.*)
They swerve off eastward ; let us follow on.
               [*Horn sounds.*
Ah ! Béziers' horn, by the clear piping note.
      [*Answers. Answer in the distance.*

Enter BÉZIERS, *attended, with falcon.*

Béziers. What of your flight, Count Raymond?
for an hour
This vagrant flies at check; she left the crow
For a mere buzzing partridge, but the bird
Did chouse thee in a ditch, my pretty dear.

                                     [Strokes his falcon.

Toulouse. Your eyette's ramage; but hast
chanced to spy
Another hawk should never leave the cadge,
A wingless creature, though from all I hear
As prone to rake and soar—Escarlamonde?

Béziers. Not since we left the walls; she was
attended
Then by the jongleur Jacques,—that idle boy,
Once Roland's friend and since he left the court
Her spaniel page.—

Foix. Now that the tomcat's gone
Whose kingly caterwauling soothed her breast
More than all human sound, she seeketh out
This tiny mewer, may—

Enter ESCARLAMONDE.

Escarlamonde. Or rather
Thrushes in elm-tree singing teach the leaves
The faint, exact re-echo of their note,

So that when autumn stoops to wed the earth
And music seeks the sun, amongst the green
Imprinted with the mavis melody
There dwell awhile full-leavèd orchestras
That softly play, but lack the master-spirit
And faint off one by one, until the last,
Mere yellow parchment, fly along the wind :
So Jacques, this bright-haired boy, the fairest
      leaf
And waxy tablet of his master's thought,
Doth ring notes in mine ear that once *he* sang ;
But you will soon forget, as youthful kind
Are wont to do, I fear me, pretty page,
You'll fly along the wind, not parchment old
But fair young lover seeking lady fair.

   Page. Ah, never, madam, could my thanks
      forget
Dear Roland.

   Foix. Hark, Lord Raymond, how he witches :
That Troubadour is half an alchemist,
I pray you bid Escarlamonde beware.

   Toulouse. You are too prone to blame ; the
      Troubadour
(I know not wherefore absent) never boiled
His golden words down in a crucible,
But poured them forth, a very Pactolus.

Foix. Whole Pactoli of words would fail to
    quell
An hundred angry knaves.
Toulouse.   You vaunt your might ;
Your service offered frankly I received,
But hold you no way to it ; by St. George !
I have here soldier-stuff shall well suffice
To turn all Montfort's surplices to shrouds.
Foix. You would be quit of me ?
Toulouse.   I said not so.
Foix. Escarlamonde was promised my reward.
Toulouse. My sister is no bale, nor merchant
    you ;
True, once I promised her, but you have piled
So many hillocks of slight difference
By money, pride and hard intolerance
Of the brave Troubadour, that as I think
A mountain stands between you and her love.
I am no longer arbiter. Count Foix,
Your fate as wooer lies alone with her.
                [*Turning to* ESCARLAMONDE.
Escarlamonde, I grant you fullest leave
To speak your soul out to the Count of Foix.
Escarlamonde. Thank you, dear brother, for
    those brother's words ;
I'll strive to fit an arrow to my speech :

Know then, Count Foix, you never had my love ;
I bore you as a yoke, because I thought
Your armed force was safety for Toulouse ;
But since my noble brother scorns such aid
(Being the lord of forests wrought in steel)
I spurn you from me as an ill-bred hound.

 Foix. What castellated towers of awful strength
Do women build of weakness !

 Escarlamonde. You spoke me often, as the
  turbaned Turk
Might to some slave girl : "Know you I could wed
Queens, Empresses, all feminine is mine?
But I choose you, the fair Escarlamonde."
Said you not so, O Prince of emptiness ?

 Foix. 'Twas but to prove my worth, for I am
  rich,
Of ancient lineage and no craven knight ;
What further merit seeks Escarlamonde
That I have not or cannot now obtain ?

 Escarlamonde. There sways no sceptre, nor
  exists the crown,
Though it were circled by the halo light
And God's eyes shone like sapphires in the gold,
Should bribe me sell my virgin coronet
Unless to save Toulouse. I see you now
Stooping to cull me—O thou million-manned

And million-moneyed nothing, get thee gone !
Go, count your gold I take this for arrow point,
Maidens love men, not beasts with gold anoint.

 Foix. Farewell, Count Raymond, we may
  chance to meet
Upon the field ; I cannot parry words
Nor do I thrust with phrases. Here ! my men !
 Toulouse. Farewell.
 Jongleur. Go in peace and hem petticoats for
  Popes.
 Falconer. Lo, yonder see they've turned the
  Royston crow.
  Toulouse. (*Addressing the company.*)
So clear an omen lacks no prophet rede—
We to their raven will play peregrine.
See, my brave fellows, see the soaring hawks
How with each stoop they claw a plumy cloud,
And sable feathers blush to crimson death !
Thus shall we meet the carrion pack of Rome ;
Be theirs the raven's fate.
 All. They die ! They die !
  [*Exeunt further afield all but* ESCARLA-
  MONDE *and* Jongleur.

   Enter a Beggar.
Beggar. A charity, sweet Lady !

Escarlamonde. Here is a silver groat, poor
  wanderer.

Beggar. A century of thanks—I bear a letter
                                    [*Gives the letter.*
From the Count de Montfort.

Escarlamonde. (*Reading.*) Sweetest Lady,
your message let Paradise into my soul ; but even
now my vileness would not dare to address your
divinity were your messenger free : alas, he was
seized by the patrolling guard just leaving my
pavilion.   He stands in danger of death ; you
alone can save him ; therefore I write and ask
you by all means to meet me at the edge of the
oak-wood, skirting our camp, at midnight.   The
bearer of this will lead you secretly thither.   My
father and the fates bind me here, or long ere this
would have been kneeling at your feet your
devoted servant,   GUY DE MONTFORT.

Escarlamonde. Ah, mad, noble Roland !
Each wind that blows fans yellower the flame
That ever glows within thee ;—Roland cap-
  tured !
My Roland ! But he needs me, and I parley ;
I'll go at once to him.   Where is the wood ?

Beggar. A long three leagues from here, my
  noble lady.

Escarlamonde. Three leagues, three miles,
 three inches, I am there.
Wilt thou conduct me?—
 Beggar.   Gladly, noble lady.
 Escarlamonde. We must be secret, for the
 Count of Foix,
Has left my brother's camp and doubtless seeks
To join Count Montfort.
 Beggar.   We'll be air to eyes,
At love's and beauty's feet the whole world lies.
         [*Exeunt.*

SCENE II.—*Crusaders' camp.*

Enter SIMON DE MONTFORT, THÉDISE, DUKE
 OF BURGUNDY, COUNT OF NEVERS, GUY
 MONTFORT, Soldiers.

Simon de Montfort. Bring forth the prisoner.

Enter ROLAND DE TRENCAVEL, *escorted by
 soldiers. He is placed opposite the dais
 where sit* SIMON DE MONTFORT *and*
 THÉDISE, *surrounded by the other barons.
 To the* Captain *of the Guard.*)

      Captain, give your report.

Captain. Most noble count, we seized the
    prisoner
At midnight, gliding outward from the camp.
    Simon de Montford. What is your name,
    whence come you, wherefore found
In the Crusaders' camp?
    Roland.   I am the knight
Roland of Trencavel ; Toulouse I left ;
But for the purpose of my journey here
I do refuse to speak.
    Simon de Montfort.   He is a knight,
Unbind him.   [ROLAND *unbound.*
           When we find an armed man
Threading our silent camp, in open war,
And when his own confession does reveal
An enemy, we slay him for a spy.
    Roland. Though bugbear death
Affright me less than aching tooth, I swear
I am no spy.
    Thédise.   Talk thou not thus of death
Who shortly wilt before thy Maker stand.
I pray, Count Montfort, let not this sinner leave
The world unchastened, for a fiery death
Does purge the soul and save eternal flames.
    Simon de Montfort. No, no, he is a brave man,
    and shall die

A gladial, knightly death.   But say, my friend,
What brought you here? your life hangs on your
     lips.

   Roland. I will not speak, though silence dig
     my grave.

   Simon de Montfort. Then, soldiers, lead him
     out.

   Guy.   One moment, stay!
Methinks I saw him at Count Raymond's
     court ;
He is the troubadour, and we should spare
One poet in ten thousand enemies.

   Thédise. Root out the pest. Count Guy, were
     those the words
Of any other baron I should guess
He was bewitched, for always singing-folk
Are satan-sprung and seek to wean men's souls
By melodies, as that terrific fiend
Lilith of old sung Adam first to sin.

   Roland. Yes, I am troubadour, but know, sir
     priest,
We poets care full little to draw men
Toward us by fear or force, those only come
Who willing come, we sell but what we have,
While your all-empty promises on earth
Will more than void celestial treasuries.

Enter MARSHALL, *announcing* COUNT OF FOIX, *followed by his men.* FOIX *approaches* DE MONTFORT *and* THÉDISE *and kneels, in token of submission.*

Marshal. The Count of Foix.

Simon de Montfort. Rise up, sir Count ; you've
    lately left Toulouse ?

Foix. I've lately left Toulouse but not, I hope,
Too late to serve the Church ; take all my lands
And vassals for the service of the Lord,
But let me serve against the heretic.

Thédise. The Church receives you as a
    wandered lamb
Back to her bosom.

Foix.   Blessed be the Lord
And the Pope Innocent.

Simon de Montfort.   You shall not lack,
Count Foix, for chance to serve most Holy
    Church
In the next battle.

Foix.   Henceforth I will strive
To cut a path to Heaven with my sword.

Simon de Montfort. Pray sit with us.
                  [FOIX *ascends dais.*
We have before us now a prisoner
From heretic Toulouse ; you may be able

E

To clear for us the purpose of his coming
Alone at midnight ; he has taken oath
Upon his knighthood (and a knight he is,
Clear written o'er and o'er,) 'twas not to spy,
But speaks no further word.

  Foix.   De Trencavel,
The troubadour, aye, well I know the man ;
A knight in truth, but nearest to a knave
Of all nobility.

  Roland. By Herakles !
Your blood shall blazon for sorrow your words
Deep in the earth, carved ready by your
   teeth,
If but the fates relent—vile renegade !

  Foix. This is Count Raymond's favourite, and
   when
The Legate Pierre was murdered at the gates
All eyes were turned his way.

  Thédise.   The murderer !
God's ways indeed are marvellous, he draws
All sinners to the stake.

  Foix. I said not Roland slew the legate Pierre,
But only that suspicion fell on him,
Being known as heretic of heretics,
As steeped in blood, a carnage roysterer,
His sword bepurpled with a thousand deaths.

Roland. Count Foix, I know not whence this
      violence
Unless it be that certain fairest dame
Preferred to yours my company.
    Thédise.   Declare,
Who slew our Legate Pierre?
    Roland. Who numbers beetles crushed beneath
      his heel?
    Thédise. When prisoners are stubborn, Holy
      Church,
As authorized by saintly Innocent,
Employs the secular arm ; you shall be tortured
Till from those lips, now ruddy but then pale
As whitest ivory, shall break confession
In fractured words of utter agony.
    Simon de Montfort. Guards, lead away the
      prisoner to watch
Till we appear ; Thédise, he shall be questioned
Before us both.
    Roland. I slew the legate Pierre.
          [Shouts and momentary confusion.
I say this nowise to escape the pain
You promise me, but that before he dies
This crowd of sodden credence led by fear
May learn how Roland hates the Christ-born
    creed.

If from the throne of God (which you aver
Lies veiled beneath the blue), Christ glideth
    down
To me all lambent with the light of Hell,
Vouchsafing an archangel diadem
And evermore the bliss of Paradise
Before God's throne, will I but worship God,
Thus shall I spit in sparks my answer back ;—
Base murderer of all things beautiful,
Get back to Heaven, blanch not our crimson
    home
With offers of an idle empery
Where serving saints doff crowns before their
    God ;
Earth-born we are, for through our human veins
Circles the music of the terrene world-—
More sweet for us, however sweet may be
The wail of harps in heavenly symphony.
Therefore avaunt, pale lamb, unless again
Thou wilt bleat forth thy life upon the cross !
And thou, Thédise, priest of the popish power,
Think not to fright me with thy Roman craft—
Long pins and screws, or racks to bend the will
Of tortured flesh to bless thy gentle creed.
I die in all defiance, but if one here
Do ever hap to see Escarlamonde,

Fair Countess of Toulouse, I hereby pray
By all he loves or ever held most dear
On earth, that bowing lowly to her feet
His lips may silent form the sacred word,
Her own four-petalled name, Escarlamonde ;
Then on their severance will an instant dwell
The breeze that haunts my tomb and softly sigh
"Escarlamonde ;" thus may she surely know
That Roland dreams of her.

>   *Guy.*   This will I do.

>   *Simon de Montfort.* De Trencavel, those
>   words have cost your life.

>   *Thédise.* Let death embrace him on the creak-
>   ing rack.

>   *Simon de Montfort.* He has confessed and
>   now deserves to die ;

But we may yet glean news from the rack's grip
That else were lost for ever.   Soldiers, lead
The prisoner forth ; pray follow us, Count Foix.

>   [*Exeunt.*

SCENE III.—*A Wood outside* MONTFORT'S
Camp. Night.

Enter GUY DE MONTFORT.

Guy. Unless my man have played me false, or
    given
The message wrongly, certes she should be here.
I sent him, hastening, before the sun
Was more than half-disc high—and all the roads
Lie open for beggars ;—sobeit through his rents
Have not peered out the soldier hid within
And wrought his capture 'ere the message
    given—
But yonder, through the trees, I surely spy
Her white against the black !

Enter ESCARLAMONDE, *with messenger, dis-
    guised as beggar.*

Escarlamonde. (*Breathless.*) Count Guy de
    Montfort !
Guy. Madame, your humblest slave.
Escarlamonde.   How fareth Roland ?
Guy. At the Council, holden this day in the
    Camp,
Roland de Trencavel confessed the murder

Of Pierre de Castelnau, and cursed the Church
Before Thédise, who fills the embassy
Of papal legate, was condemned to die
And bad me, in some strange, gold-woven phrase,
To say before you but your name from him,
" Escarlamonde."—

   Escarlamonde.   He lives ! he lives !
He cannot die !—now kill me with the truth—
They've murdered him ?—

   Guy.   I think he is not dead,
But it may be that holding back his breath
Under the torture as did—

   Escarlamonde.   If he be dead,
Then is the world my living tomb, those stars
Mere gilded nails to penn a misery
Would reach beyond them into utmost space
And wed with chaos.

   Guy. And so you love him, lady? when I heard
Roland before that crowd of angry looks
Declare such bright defiance, o'er my mind
Shuddered the thought he must be deep in love;
Then at the last his message, " Whisper once
Her name Escarlamonde," brought home to me
Whence light did flood his soul; but at Toulouse
He did deceive me basely, never word
To all my wild avowals of a love

For your bright star ; ha ! how the rogue within
Must have built towers of proud contempt for me
Who came a stranger to the prisoned dove
He kept in open cage and thought to lure
So sweet a prey from home——

 Escarlamonde. (Producing GUY'S *letter.*) You
   sent me this,
And said here I might save him : I am here,
Ready to pay his safety with such coin
As molten in one crucible of pain
Body and soul may give.   What shall I do?
 Guy. (Falling on his knees.) Ah ! let the silent
   ocean of my love
But drink his furnace flame !

 Escarlamonde.   I madly wrote
To please his madness what I fear you hold
A letter of love to you, it bore your name :
But those words, "wait and watch," addressed
   to you,
A stranger hardly seen, were the true sign
Of utter, deep devotion to the man
Whose worshipper I pride myself.

 Guy.   But now,
He may be dead.

 Escarlamonde. [*Showing a dagger.*] This will
   soon rend the veil

Hiding his dead life from my living death—
Speak, what to save him?

  Guy. (*Still on his knees.*) Ah ! Escarlamonde,
Fly but with me and I will be the slave
Of your contempt for ever, for my love
Beyond you sees but darkness, and behind
One sandy desert.

  Escarlamonde.   Silence, and arise ;
Unless you straightway point me out the road
That leads to Roland's rescue (if he lives)
I will to your father's camp, and on my knees
Offer this life for Roland and declare,
Viper, thy slimy meanness ; make thy choice.

  Guy. Escarlamonde, your love had made of
    me
A giant among men, your scorn has rased
My manhood to the dust, not killed a love
Which is immortal, larger than myself,
Nescient of human law and uncontrolled
By the swift accident of earthly change.
I am bereptiled and must therefore crawl
True to the coiling kind ;—If I procure
Roland's salvation, you must pledge your word
For my reception in Toulouse and grant
Free leave to woo you, if I may not win.

  Escarlamonde. This all I swear.

Guy.   Good, then return with speed,
Inform Count Raymond that with all my men
(My private guard) I do desert for him.
Let a strong force arrange to-night a march
And come upon our camp in the early hours.
Roland is guarded in the middle tent
Near my pavilion ; I will drug his guard,
And when the battle rages, with my men
Seize Roland and escape.

Escarlamonde.   O model knave,
It is a compact sworn for Roland's sake.

Guy. I kiss the hand that laid me in the dust,
Then taught those lips to curl at my disgrace.

Escarlamonde. Farewell, Count Montfort, we
        shall meet again.

Guy. Farewell, fair ringlets that have wove my
        chain.   [*Exeunt.*

SCENE IV.—ROLAND'S *prison in the Camp of
        the Crusaders.* ROLAND *discovered prostrate
        on a low bed. Midnight.*

Enter GUY DE MONTFORT.

*Guy. In a low whisper; the whole scene is
        carried on in undertones.*)
Roland de Trencavel, awake, 'tis I,

Younger de Montfort.

Roland. (*In a weak whisper.*) What would
    you with me? let me lie in peace :
You and the rack have well-nigh made my sleep
Eternal, as ere long they doubtless will.

Guy. You suffered, but my utmost credit went
To shield you from the priest ; yea, even now
My father's name alone prevents suspicion
Choking his son.

Roland.   Perchance you did your most.

Guy. If then I did my most I since achieved
A more than most will link your sundered bones.
I've seen Escarlamonde.

Roland.   You've seen the sun
At midnight, or the moon lit on an oak
To rest herself : Montfort, you are a dream.

Guy. No dream, true blood and flesh in
    burnished steel,
Ready to wreak your rescue ; but I think
You slip from promises, the purpose won,
Like bees from drained iris.

Roland. (*Half arisen.*)   What mean you?
                      [*Aside.*

I think he is a dream, and yet the voice
And all the presence so bespeak the man
I once did know for Montfort, that my eyes

Can scarce believe they're closed.

Guy. (*Advancing to the bed-side and tendering
his gauntleted hand to* ROLAND, *sitting up.*)

                                 Here, doubt no more ;
Marshal the senses by the sensitive :
But you, I fear, are drawn
So many ways with pain that what was once
Essential matter of intelligence
Is grown but perfume clinging round the wreck
Of shivered memory. '

Roland. (*Rising with difficulty to his feet, by
help of* GUY DE MONTFORT'S *hand.*)

                              How come you here ?
Where is the guard ?

Guy.   My father's name and fame
Set iron bolts a-tremble, and the guard
Cushion the ground for footstool to my feet ;
I come to save your life, but first will bring
Face to your face some trifles light as down
Weighty as lead to me.

Roland.   Say on.

Guy.   One day,
Not a week old, we met within Toulouse,
And holding you for trusty friend, I bared
The secret of my heart to friendship's ear,
And asked your help, having once given you mine

In such a crisis. You then promised me
A fair return, that you would steadfast strive
To win for me until the war were done
The love of bright, bright blue Escarlamonde.

Roland. I promised, and so far as in me lay,
Performed.

    Guy.   Why did you not reveal your love,
Lit at the same torch ?

    Roland.   Because I had sworn
To help you as you once had holpen me,
And well I knew that once her fairness felt,
Hope lit and then extinguished, it would kill
       you
More surely than the band of ruffians
Had sped me to my death but for your aid
In Paris long ago.

    Guy.   You rightly read
My trembling heart.

    Roland. It throbbed through all your speech,
Therefore I built as far as words could build
Your favour with Escarlamonde, and now,
Had I not met the evil chance of night,
Should be again within Toulouse's walls
Which I shall never see again.

    Guy.   You spoke
No selfish word of love ?

Roland.   No single sigh
Breathed mute avowal through my prison lips.

   Guy. Then will I save your life and bring
     you back
Safely to Raymond's court.

   Roland.   *You* bring me back
To Raymond's court !

   Guy.   Yes, though the blazoned gates
Of proud Toulouse see the all-proudest son
Of lion father crawl there on his knees.

   Roland. What means this ? How can Mont-
     fort seek Toulouse ?

   Guy. Hearken and hear a calendar of death.
When last we met at Raymond's court, my name
Glinted the sun-ray back with ten-fold light ;
Honour and pride did perch upon my crest
Like eagles on their mountain pinnacle,
Undaunted, unapproached ; then none had dared
To but rebuke me, smiling, for a fault
My doing had made virtue.   Thus I shone
Until the stars gave me another sun,
A fearsome orb—
Quite full of flame and fierce malignity,
Of perfect splendour which did concentrate,
Such dire, effective lightnings in her gaze
As turned me to decay (thus often lakes,

Lying beneath the intolerable heat
Of some vast tropic constellation, shrink
Until the crystal mantle of their waves
Be rent asunder and beneath reveal
Miasma plains of mud); mine is their fate ;
I rot beneath the fire of this new sun,
Escarlamonde, all creviced, all sucked-up
And burned to ruin with eternal love
Of her infernal fairness ;—all has gone—
Honour, religion, country, father, fame ;
Long, lean-necked vultures probe their prostrate
      corse, ·
And fleeing eagles shriek along the wind.
              [*Distant sounds of battle.*

  Roland. If we escape I'm anchored to my
    oath,
Of loyal love service.
  Guy.   I must away
Gather my trusted men.
  Roland.   Ah, I forgot
To question the salvation of my life.
  Guy. In truth I should have told you—an
    attack
From Raymond we devised—hear the first
    breath—
I join and simulate resistance, then

In the red cloak and black of warful knight
Hither return, first slay the amazed guard,
Then skirt with you the battle and take horse
Straight for Toulouse. Farewell, we meet again.
[*Exit* GUY DE MONTFORT.
Roland. Alive again ! I who so deeply drank
Of death's deep-poppied bowl that all the world
Seemed to my distant senses as a star,
Buried in blue to gazer upon earth.
[*Shouts and clash of battle.*
Escarlamonde ! then once again these eyes
May steal the lyrics sleeping in thy smile,
And draw gold rapture from thy floating hair.
Ah ! I could live for ages on the life
Of seeing her alive ! Ah ! but to know
She breathed yet and with her amber sighs
Turned all the other winds to wed the south.
[*Tumult.*
And northern Montfort loves ; his frosty soul
Once melted in the meeting of her eyes
Now flows a torrent to the cataract. [*Tumult.*
I might plead for him all the years of earth
And every word but make her love him less.
[*Tumult.*
I pity him to lowest similes,
For well I know she loves me utterly

With a far richer treasury of love
Than we can reach the spending on the earth.

Enter GUY DE MONTFORT.

Guy. Come, lean on me, I have a horse for
    you,
Or mine for both, if still you are too weak
To sit in saddle.   [*Exeunt.*

END OF ACT II.

ACT III.

SCENE I.—*Toulouse. The Great Banquet-Hall.*
    RAYMOND, Count *of* Toulouse, ROLAND
    DE TRENCAVEL, BEZIERS, COMMINGES,
    ESCARLAMONDE, *other Barons, Retainers,*
    discovered.

Raymond. Fill all the cups with reddest wine
    and drink
Our Roland back again, and Guy de Montfort
Who saved his life and thereby gains our love.
      [*All drink.*

F

And what of the escape? why did you venture,
Roland, so near their camp?

  Roland.   My lord, to judge
Their numbers and position ; by ill-chance
A log that smouldered in a watch-fire
Flared up as I passed by and thus revealed
My presence to their guard of fifty ;—but
Count Guy will better tell of our escape
After my trial, for 'twas he that planned it—
He only—and his name our talisman.

  Guy. First let me thank the noble Count
    Raymond
(And all my thanks do leave me deep in debt),
For his so princely welcome in Toulouse
And swift acceptance of such services
As I may render ; but for our escape
'Twas easy managed, I but gave the alarm
Of your attack, and rushing foremost forth,
Roland and I, with fifty of my men,
Did join your Albigensians and retreat.

  Raymond. Again all welcome.

  Escarlamonde.   Brother mine, how pale
Is Roland since he left us !

  Roland.   Yes, my cheeks
Caught pallor from their company, but soon
Toulouse and her red wine will re-imprint

The hue that used to haunt them.

    Escarlamonde. (*Aside to* ROLAND). Will you
        meet me
To-morrow in the garden, for I have
A world of words to whisper you alone ?

    Guy. (*Aside to* ROLAND). Roland, methinks
        you strangely keep your faith.

    Roland. How can I hinder her ?

    Guy.   Most easefully,
Were it but with your will.

    Raymond.   I pray you cease
Disputes, and rather let our Roland sing
Some song of his to cheer us.

    Guy.   Will not Count Roland
Sing the gay verse he penned to please a maid
Once in Anjou ; they say she died of love
For his bright eyes.

    Roland.   I know not what you mean.
I have made many songs for many maids—
It is my only craft—but which an one
Died for my love I know not ; nor I think
Does the Count Guy, but rather that he will
Goad from me hasteful words and cast a sully,
So far as in him lies, on my fair fame.

    Raymond. Silence, I pray ; once more fill high
        the cups,

And let us drink the death to all our foes,

                       [*To* COUNT GUY.

Save, for your sake, your father's !

  Guy.   Would he were

Slain by my hand ; ah, let him but appear

Within these walls, and if the fates be fair

I shall transpierce him.

  All.   Well said ! Well said !

  Raymond. For those words you shall guard
       our palace gate,

And here the voucher of my earnestness,

The master-key.   [*Gives golden key.*

  Roland.   Does no command fall mine

As once, Prince Raymond?

  Escarlamonde.   Roland must allow

His weary body rest ere it can match

Imperious spirit promptings.

  Raymond.   Truly said,

Countess, my sister ; Roland, thou shalt lie

Here in the palace, till Escarlamonde

Our doctoress do grant thee fully cured,

Able to wield again thy burnished blade

That animates with death the servant-spears

Crowding behind ; (*Rising*), now let us part, and
       pray

The radiant gods of bright antiquity

To bear our cause at heart.   Let Count de Mont-
    fort
Bè shewn the chamber destined for his use.

                         [*Exeunt.*

SCENE II.—*The Palace garden.*

Enter ROLAND *and* ESCARLAMONDE : *they
walk up and down.*

Roland. You know I love you and shall always
    love.

Escarlamonde. You see I ever love you and
    shall love.

Roland. Wherefore, when now each has the
    other's faith
Eternal, seek you more?

Escarlamonde.   I will to know
Your sudden change from open adoration
To distant, cold eye-worship.

Roland.   Loveliest one
My honour stands before a closer bond.

Escarlamonde. Your honour ! is it therefore
    honourable
To steal away both heart and soul, and then,
In lofty fashion pleading your honour, ban

Me all my life and death to misery !
Ah, Roland let us live back to the past !
  Roland. Could I outlive my promise to Count
      Guy,
Which as a net thrown forward from the past
Snares all my future in its coilèd web,
Could I but grasp anew the floating hair
Of Destiny, and drag her back again
To the clear hill-top whence we viewed the world
Glittering below, then wer'st thou surely mine ;
But now—no words nor deeds can fill the chasm
Between us blasted to eternity.
  Escarlamonde. Farewell, farewell for ever, now
      I will
Seek some old turret-cloister and alone
Dream a long, stationary dream of thee
As once a year ago thy meeting smile
Builded for me my share of Paradise.   [*Weeps.*

     Enter GUY DE MONTFORT.

  Guy. Vile, perjured hound ! where is your
      pledged faith
Never again to court Escarlamonde ?
  Roland. No man can be another man in love,
Only himself, therefore I said adieu
For ever to Escarlamonde ; you have

The longed-for haven open and can urge
Alone your suit, but of that bitter speech
Our judges hang beside us.   [*They draw.*
  Guy. So, let us fight, and by your speedy death
I will disclose to fair Escarlamonde
How more than you I love her.
    Escarlamonde.   Should your boast
Chance true, and Roland fall, I could not hate
    you,
Love him, one whit the more.
      [*Exit* ESCARLAMONDE. ROLAND *and* GUY
        DE MONTFORT *fight, but are arrested by
        sounds of battle.*

      Enter SIMON DE MONTFORT, DE FOIX,
          and Crusaders.

  Roland.   Stay, Guy de Montfort!
You left the walls unguarded, and behold
Your work.   Ha ! Count of Foix, have at you !
  Foix. Stand back, my men, while I chastise
      this knave. [ROLAND *and* DE FOIX *fight.*
  Guy. Loveless and lonely I will drown myself
In living blood.   A Montfort ! A Montfort !
      [*Rushes into the mêlée and is killed.* ROLAND
        *falls wounded—the battle moves onwards
        —flames burst from the palace windows.*

Roland. Escarlamonde ! Escarlamonde !

Enter ESCARLAMONDE *from the Palace.*

The utter joy of thy fair vision
Makes of this moment an eternity :
When I am gone those eyes will think of me
Tearfully sometimes ?
    Escarlamonde. You left me once and went but
        fifty miles ;
My heart bled out the inches of your way :
And now, my darling, when your path is set
Much farther off, among the yellow stars,
Shall I not follow?
    Roland. Escarlamonde, I think no other man
Has ever slept in such a bed of bliss
As where your soft words lay me ; let us pass
Starward together, for I feel my soul
Disanchored ride upon thin waves of air. [*Dies.*
    Escarlamonde. Farewell, farewell, forever to
      the world.   [*Stabs herself. Dies.*

FINIS.

1887.

OFF THE HARBOUR OF MESSINA.

1586.

SCENE.—*Off the Harbour of Messina.*

The Cabin of SCIPIO CICALA.[1]

Scipio Cicala. My own dear mother, here at
    length you stand
On Islam's soil ; yon puling Spanish cur
May bite his mangy paws for your return
In coward impotence ; but tell me why
Lucretia comes not with you? I received
Your letter saying she was ill, but so
I knew it was not—had the Viceroy sent
Such an excuse, Viceroy by now he were
With flames and cinders for Viceroyalty.
    Countess Cicala. She was indeed too weak to
    leave her bed :
Your nephew, called Scipio after you,

---

[1] For an account of Cicala *see* Creasy's " History of the
Ottoman Turks."

Is now but three weeks old. "Tell him," she said,
" How all my thoughts are his, and that my child
Shall learn my brother's life for history :
Often," she said, " I look toward the east
Down the broad stretch of sea that flows to where
Constantinople rises from the waves,
Feeling I'm Scipio's guest, to whom the sea
Is all one blue-eyed slave."

   Scipio Cicala.   So let it be ;
Sweet sister's flattery covers as a veil
The Christian hate ; tell her, if e'er her son
Feel as I felt, and would return again
To Islam's faith, let him be sent to me,
And I will carve him out in the steep rock
That leads to fame those earliest vantage-steps,
More difficult than any after them.
Tell me, dear mother, during all the years
That have rolled over us, since father and I
Set sail for Djerbé, where he found his death
And I my life, has the Sicilian air
Blown gently on my mother's gentleness ?

   Countess Cicala. Two years I mourned your
       father and my son
(For you, I thought, were also dead, or worse—
Sold as a slave), I never left my home
Until the radiant news came from the East—

The Padischah had smiled upon my son,
My own, my beautiful (what help had he ?)—
Then I went forth and sought the Christian Church
To thank the Christian God, but all the words
My heart could find were "Allah Merciful,"
"Prophet, I thank thee, lover of the brave" ;—
Then back again to "Allah Merciful."

    Scipio Cicala. News travels slowly from the
        East, except
The news of war.

    Countess Cicala. Aye, it was many months
Before I heard again that you had topped
So many Moslem heads and stood at last
Yourself proud Aga of Janissaries.

    Scipio Cicala. My upward path was easy with
        the sun
Of great Solyman shining.

    Countess Cicala.   Afterwards,
Again there fell a silence ; "He is dead
Perhaps," I thought, and every colourless day
Led me a further step into the tomb.
I trembled, for I knew the perilous height
Where you were standing was enclosed round
With the snake's circle of the scimitar,
Most deadly treacherous.

    Scipio Cicala.   I had a charm

To soothe such snakes asleep, one little word,
"The Bosphorus."

    Countess Cicala.   And then?

    Scipio Cicala.   I sought a bride,
And found Irene, daughter of the Sot,[1]
Granddaughter of the mighty Padischah,
Sister of Amurath, and thus equipped
I dared forsake the town.

    Countess Cicala.   You left your bride
With but your name to husband?

    Scipio Cicala.   Choice was none,
The Persian thunder rumbled.

    Countess Cicala.   And she wept?

    Scipio Cicala. Mayhap she wept.

    Countess Cicala.   You won the victory,
And then she dried her tears to know you safe,
Sweet daughter mine.

    Scipio Cicala.   Oh! 'twas a bloody field![2]
We fell upon them at the dead of the night;
Their camp was black,—scarcely a glimmering
     light
Shewed us their tents,—they slumbered,—with a
     rush

---

[1] Sultan Selim the *Sot* son of Solyman. This epithet is applied to Selim by the historians of his own country.

[2] The Battle of the Torches is here described.

We were upon them, and the fiery glare
Of forty thousand torches struck a dread
Of demon's to their heart, before they knew
That we were men they were not men them-
      selves—
Corpses or cowards—oh ! 'twas a butchery
To make the earth spue blood, myself I was
A gardener lopping mandrake ; [1] one alone
Of all the crew dared face me, he had left
The battle, mounted for retreat ; he was
A squadron officer ; he drew rein and turned,
Viewed me, dismounted, and our married steel
Struck sparks like fire-flies dancing in the night.
He fell at last,—I had gashed his forehead deep,
Blinded his eyes with blood ; I knelt by his side,
Saying, " Confess the faith and save your days—
Mahomet and Amurath the Padischah
And one God over all ;" he gaspèd forth,
" Ormuzd Ahriman and the Schah-in-Schah."

   Countess Cicala. You spared him, Scipio ?
   Scipio Cicala.   I propped his head
Upon a stone, bound up his wound, and sought
Again the garden.
   Countess Cicala. There spoke my own brave son.

  [1] *Mandrake.* This plant was supposed to shriek when
plucked.

Scipio Cicalo. I think it was my mother, not
    her son
That spared the Persian ; mercy's a weakling
    word,
Lacks to my alphabet ; before nor since
I never wavered.
    Countess Cicala.   Now you are advanced
To Lord High Admiral of the Crescent fleets?
    Scipio Cicala. Aye, they thought my mood
Were more in tune with pirates and with foes :
They missed too many heads when I was Aga,
So the "son of a slave"[1] wrote with his own
    great hand
My appointment to be Capitan Pascha
Of all the fleets, gilded the wording well,
Called mine "amphibious glory,"[2] and a host
Of such strange words, all this the learnèd said
Was poetry ; if this be poetry,
Then poetry was useless even to mask
The dread they felt to see me once again
(I mean the eunuchs and the courtly crowd)

---

[1] The "Son of a Slave" is a term by which the Turkish
people often speak of the Sultan.   Creasy, "History of
the Ottoman Turks."

[2] The love and practice of poetry is traditional in the
House of Othman.

Aga of them and of Janissaries.

    Countess Cicala. The sun is sinking—galloping
        to the west .
To end my little day ; oh ! the gun will sound,
Calling me back to death and Sicily,
It booms already in my heart.

    [*Taking a small golden cross from her neck.*
                         This cross
                [*Giving it to* CICALA.
Your father gave me on our wedding day ;
I swore to wear it while I loved him best
Of all the world ; now keep it for my sake,
Not as religious sign,—since I was seized,   .
Trembling, a prey at Modon, I have felt
Sufficient weight of sorrow to deserve
This as *my* symbol also . . . . . .
Wear it, my son, my darling, for my sake.
We shall not meet again, it cannot be,
For I am old and you too near the heart
Of the throbbing world ; mayhap when I am dead,
And you are laid with glory in the grave,
Mayhap, though I have left the Prophet's faith,
Such perfect love is mine that Christ will build
A little bridge across to Mahomet's heaven,
That I may pass along, and peeping through
The brilliant chinks, have but one glimpse of you

Throned on the white and green ; I will not ask
More than to *see* you once, for my gray hairs⁻
Were all ajar in Mahomet's glorious heaven.

    Scipio Cicala. But, mother dear, in Jesus' Para-
        dise
You will be young, your locks run gold again
As once they did.

    Countess Cicala. No, I have grown too old
        upon the earth
For even Heaven to make me young again,
And *happy—never* in the Christian Heaven,
When all my thoughts are twined about my son.

    Scipio Cicala. Then come with me and join
        the Prophet's faith.

    Countess Cicala. I cannot leave Lucretia
To be the victim of the Christian rage ;
They well might murder her to prove the hate
They bear to Islam.

    Scipio Cicala.   By the Prophet's beard,
I'll burn Messina down, I'll rake the coast
For leagues and leagues, as once before I did
When they refused me sight of you ; I'll stamp
The Viceroy and his princedom into dust !

                      [*Calls to the patrol.*

What ho there !

    Captain of the Patrol. My lord ?—

Countess Cicala. And little sister, her whose
    hand you held
A tiny boy, and said, "Lucretia,
I am your brother, I am stronger far
Than you can ever be, and therefore I
Will guard you through the world, and if any dare
So much as look unkindly—he must die."
'Twas thus you lisped in the old, early time,
And now?
    Scipio Cicala. Now, I am still her brother.
                           [*Gun sounds on shore.*
    Countess Cicala. My recall, the sunset gun : I
    will not weep,
No, I am rich for ever from to-day,
    [*Hides her face, then suddenly throws her
    arms round his neck and embraces him
    silently.*
    Scipio Cicala. Farewell, my mother.
    [*She enters the skiff and disappears at the
    entrance to the harbour of Messina.
    When she is out of sight,* SCIPIO CICALA
    turns to the Captain of the Patrol.*
Weigh anchor, steer to the east, set free
What sailors are in chains, and give them wine.
    Captain of the Watch. (*Aside.*) A miracle !
    Scipio Cicala.   You said ?
                      G

Captain of the Watch.   Nothing, my Lord.

Scipio Cicala. (*To the Sailors standing round.*)
Hang me this fellow to the mast.

Sailors.   Yes, my Lord.

THE END.

THE LEGEND OF ST. AGNES.

THROUGH the spacious streets of Rome do you
    see
  Yon sylph-slim damosel tripping alone—
Alone, or is it her ancient nurse
  Stumbling behind over every stone?

(Rome is herself and the eagle wings
  Yet darken the uttermost ends of earth,
But the humble manger of Bethlehem
  Has given the God Son birth,

Has given him birth and the death he craved,
  From the mountain peak he has cried,
" Whosoever will come to my Father's House
  Shall in nowise be denied.")

Agnes is yet but a little child,
  For Summer has scarcely had time to alight
In gold on her hair, or skies to lend azure,
  Or Winter to dress her in white :

She is hastening homeward, her lesson is over :
    Thinking is she, now free of control,
Of one whom she loves with her white with her
        golden
    With her violet eyes, with her soul.

" Good-morrow, I wish you, Agnes nobilis,
    Agnes venusta, Agnes columba,
Agnes animula, long have I loved you,
    Rome have I sought for you days without
        number."

But *him* she loves not, she fawn-like shrinketh
    (O nurse, are the ways so steep ?)
" Sir ,I know you not, I am homeward hasting,
    I fain my path would keep."

" I am Procopius, son of Symphorion
    Prefect of Rome, and I will not leave you,
Ere you have promised to wed me, my Father
    Says as a daughter he will receive you."

" I thank you, Procopius, my bridegroom is
        chosen,
    Choose for yourself some fairer woman."
" Who," said Procopius, "who is the bridegroom ?
    You shall be my bride or the bride of no man :

" Purple and slaves and swift-rolling chariots,
    All these are mine and whoever you are,
Bridegroom elected, better you have not."—
    Said Agnes, " Better far."

" Mehercule ! maiden, I pray you to to tell me
    Who is the man, does he dwell in Rome?
I fain would see him—see him and slay him."
    Said the virgin, " Yonder his home."

Skyward she pointed, Procopius staring
    From her tiny finger-tip, stared till his eyes,
Weary of roaming immensity,
    Fell back into her eyes.

Then all the madness flowed in upon him,
    " O thou art mine, I swear it shall be ;
If you love me not, my love shall suffice us ;"
    Said Agnes, " You are not He.

" He is far greater, better and wiser,
    Perfect is he, see his blood in my·cheeks [1]
Glows at your insult, leave me, unhand me,
    Victim of death ! "   Procopius seeks

[1] Sanguis ejus ornavit genas meas.—*Acts of St. Agnes.*

Vainly the word or the strength to detain her,
    He leans on the wall with her scorn in his
        heart ;
They found him at nightfall a raving madness ;
    " He is far beyond the sphere of our art,"

Whisper the doctors, "she only can save
        him."
    " Will you murder or marry my only son ? "
Thunders the prefect, " I cannot ; I will not," [1]
Answers heroic the little one.

" You will not marry him, *certes*, none other
    Bridegroom but mine shall achieve your
        desire ;
Shut out from the world and a virgin for ever
    You shall guard the Vestal Fire."

" O pave your streets with your gods," said the
        maiden,
    " Stone and bronze were of use to tread —
My God lives yonder," (she pointed to Heaven),
    " Yours were of earth and were always dead."

[1] Non possum, non volo.—*Acts of St. Agnes.*

" Christian accursed ! vilest blasphemer!
   " Witch Galilean ! Guards, bear her hence !
Vesta will none of her, godly Priapus
   Shall show her a larger lenience."

    *   *   *   *   *   *

    *   *   *   *   *   *

    *   *   *   *   *   *

O 'twas a sight to turn day to night
   As white, with her golden hair that hung
   The while they walked their feet among,
The child was swayed to left to right,
   Jostled, bespattered by the rude,
   The pagan Roman multitude,
And as they passed the crier cried,
" See the magician that denied
The gods of Rome, lo, now we bear her
Where every man of you may share her."

    *   *   *   *   *   *

And now she stands in the nameless place,
   Face to face with a worse than death,
She trembles not, she has faith in her Lover.
   " Tear off her robe," the centurion saith.

It falls in pieces, but all of the golden
   Curls will defend her a moment's space,

Till from the mystical air that is round her,
  Sweet Agnes is wrapped in a garment of grace.

This is a tissue wrought for the angels,
  Clothèd in heaven she raises her eyes,
Silently thanking her royal bridegroom ;
  None dare approach her save him who defies

The very Son of his God, 'tis Procopius,
  Madly he cries, "Now at last she is mine ;"
He rushes to seize her, but rolls on the marble,
  Shivered to dust by a shaft divine.

And now see the Prefect, shaken with sobbing,
  (O a strong man's tears are a terrible thing,)
He kneels at her feet, "O pray to your Lover,
  Pray that my son back to life he may bring."

"Leave me alone with him, then I will ask him ;"
  (Could her blanchèd lips be denied ?)
Returning, they find him from Hell back-wafted,
  A miracle, at her side.

And here the very words of the history
  Burst into scarlet to speak of their shame ;—

Father and son without help or thanksgiving
  Slink to their kennel. " Come, kindle a flame,"

Shouts the centurion, "Guards, bear the faggots,"
  Echoes the crowd, " Let her burn, let her
    burn,"
Vainly Aspasius [1] (like Pilate before him)-
  Strives the blind flow of their frenzy to turn.

Tied to the stake, see the tiny maiden,
  Like an opening flower spread the flames of
    her pyre ;
Scatheless and radiant she stands in the centre,
  Peerless Anemone, petalled with fire :

Pressing around her the Roman vainglorious
  With a gust of the furnace withers away ;
For an hour she beholds from her magic circle
  The powers of the pagan world at bay.

[1] Aspasias was vicar of Rome. Tillemont is of opinion
that this office was created under Diocletian. The
vicar's judgments were without appeal. Upon the de-
parture of Symphorion he doubtless occupied the place
of chief magistrate, which suggests the parallel of Pontius
Pilate.

Then at their flames and her flowers sun-setting
  She raises her blue inestimate orbs
Up to the zenith and prays to her Lover,
  "As the ambient air these flames absorbs

"So may I now pass to the bliss of thy dwelling
  If so it seems good to thee, good my Lord."
Is there God or man could resist such a pleading?
  Nor man, nor God, with a glittering sword,

Calling on Mars, on Priapus, on Pluto,
  Blindly the soldier strikes at her breast :
She is gone, she is passed to the arms of her
    bridegroom,
  Youngest of saints, child queen of the blest !

And this is thy legend on earth, O St. Agnes ;
  It is all too fair and too blue for my rhyme,
I would claim one boon of the Lord, thy Lover,
  Crave to adore thee in heavenly clime.

Then were my song and my saying triumphant,
  Limitless, perfect and pure as thou art ;
Here upon earth I but love thee and follow,
  Counting thy steps by the beats of my heart.

SONNET TO WORDSWORTH.

" ONE touch of Nature makes the whole world
    kin,"
And thou wast Nature's self, ambassador
To bear the message that the Mantuan bore ;
Therefore we love thee, whether we have been
Bred among bricks or know the beech-tree's
    sheen.
Hearken ! 'tis Wordsworth speaks, his lips out-
    pour
The vasty sum of things ; hearken once more,
Or did the field-mouse chirrup on the green ?
Alone thou lookest from yon Julian peak,
The winds are holding silence round thy head,
The eagle passes downward to his bed
Weary of heaven. Ah ! vain indeed to seek
The path among the clouds that thou didst
    tread,
Athwart the chasm thou canst with Shakespeare
    speak.

TO SOME SUNFLOWERS

SEEN WITH THEIR HEADS TURNED AWAY
FROM THE SUN. GERMANY, 1892.

SUN-FLOWERS, sun-flowers,
   Why seek ye not the sun?
Ye cannot tell how many hours
   He has gilded on his round.

. We are tired of peeping,
   We would be sleeping
Beneath the quiet ground ;
Sun-flowers, sun-flowers,
   All is not well with ye ;
Of old throughout September's showers
   Ye waited patiently.

'Tis true, O poet,
   But well ye know it,
We are but mortals, a god is he,
   Days long we waited
   Bestormed, belated,

Nor ever a glimpse of his face did see—
  And now that he's waking,
  His couch forsaking,
  Our heads are aching,
  Our brown eyes dim—
Oh ! we'd be creeping
  Earthward and sleeping
Rescued from heaven and from memories
    of him.

THE QUESTION.

Is it a leaf or a butterfly
That flutters there against the sky,
Sometimes it seems to live,
Sometimes to die
Sinking earthward helplessly?
It is a leaf and a butterfly,
Living and dead like earth and sky;
All things thou seemst to see
Are as this leafy butterfly
Mere phases of thy phantasy.

THE LUNATIC.

THE moon is veiled to-night,
She shines behind a cloud,
She shines for other's sight.
I do not care to pass
When the moon has ceased to shine ;
The moon is veiled, alas,
Yet will I wander on
Through streets or through the woods,
Although the moon be gone. .
When the early morning cleared
The misty things of night,
Then sometimes she appeared,—
She shone not, being dead,
She was so pale and faint,
"Good-bye," was all she said—
But what more could she say,
Poor victim of the sun ?
I hate his garish day.

SONNET ON "THE SORCERESS," PORTRAIT BY GRAHAM ROBERTSON.

SHE stands amid the fir-trees while the light
Of the ever-evening sun about her shed
Makes ruddier the russet of her head :
Sister of Vivian and of Circe bright,
She waits among the woods upon the dead,
Nearing her now, in vain, the silly sprite,
The ingenuous goblin, they have tricked and fled,
For them her arms are blue with aconite.
Thou art not human, essence of the air,
Bred on the earth long ere the age of man,
Protean sorceress thou standest there,
Woman a moment, in a moment's span
Serpent again; change not, no dæmon can
Be better dæmon than a woman fair.

MNEMOSYNE.

Now many an age is buried
  Since first thou rosest for me
Where I stood in the June-green coppice
  Gazing outward on the sea.
Blue were the morning billows,
  White gleamed the mariner's sails,
The tufted grass was playing
  With the edgeless western gales.
Meward the Tritons bore thee,
  Poised on thy roseate shell,
Pendant thy gold hair glittered,
  Thy sea-eyes wrought their spell.
I did not dare to greet thee,
  Thou wast so fearful fair :
" Steer to his heart," thou saidest,
  " I will make harbour there."
 *   *   *   *   *   *   *

The thousand years are over,
  My spear is split in twain,

Dinted are hauberk and helmet,
    And I have fought in vain.
Thou wast nor goddess nor dæmon
    Thou wast an Eidolon,
The shadow of something perfect
    Breathing a malison.
I know I shall never know it,
    I shall never know of thee
More than the right eternal
    To thy bright agony.
And now though the God of Heaven
    Made gift of myself to me,
I would choose to meet thee gliding
    Again on the morning sea.

A SONNET OF POISONS.

WITCH, come thou forth from out the ebony
    night
Bearing us armfuls o' th' infernal flowers,
Enough of life enarsenaled with hours
Soul-murderers all, come wreath the aconite,
Fit coronal for this dark brow of ours.
Sweet witch, come forth, and let thy kiss alight
Cold on our lips, that when we meet the powers
Of hell we may find favour in their sight.
Foul witch ! thy deaths are dead, see where they
    lie,
Monkshood, the nightshade, withered at our feet,
Yea, and thyself, the very witch, art dead
That kissed our lips more puissant poisoned
Than thy dead deadly lips ; come, Daphne, greet
Us with thy pitying smile, we fain would die.

THE DREAM.

LAST night as I lay a-dreaming
  Alone in my frozen bed
Meseemèd I caught the gleaming
  Of thine imperial head.
Then me from my place upraising
  (For I sat far away)
I thridded the crowd agazing
  On the players at their play.
But when our eyes ameeting
  I was piercèd by the gleam,
I knew by thy sweet smile greeting
  In my dream it was a dream.

A BALLAD OF BIRDS.

HIGH, high above the earth the happy birds
Are passing with the sunlight on their wings.
    Oh, eastward ho ! or westward ho !
    Ye know nor heed not whither ye go.
      Above the clouds the sky is fair
      The sun is shining everywhere,
      Why should ye care?
      Oh to be of you,
      Oh to be with you,
    For ever roaming hither, thither,
    Sweet birds, for ever careless whither ;
Oh to be free from myself in the air !

    *   *   *   *   *
    *   *   *   *   *

    High, high above the earth we are looking down
    On quiet hamlet or on busy town,
    All things we see, dew glittering on the rose,
    Dew or a tear, who knows?

We see but do not know.
Oh, eastward ho ! or westward ho !
We know nor care not whither we go.
Above the clouds the sky is fair,
The sun is shining everywhere,
Why should we care?
For ever roaming hither, thither,
We birds, for ever careless whither
Oh, I am of you,
Oh, I am with you,
Oh, I am free from myself in the air.

THE GALLERY.

I MET thee in the gallery,
  Glittering Medusawise,
I knew that thou wast seeking me
  With those Medusa eyes.
I did not dare to look, but fled,
  I fled—and felt thee smile :
It meant "is not his *body* dead"?
  Thy damnèd pitying smile.
Oh ! thou that drawest men as the moon
  The billows of the sea,
Shrink to a toad—God grant the boon—·
  That in a rock with thee
I, only I, may dwell and say,
  " These fearful crimson eyes,
This platèd back, this glairy clay,
  These are my paradise,
For these are *thee* and thou art mine ;
  Crash Athens, Egypt, Rome,
I drink thy reptile blood like wine,
  Thy toad's heart is my home."

TO A MARBLE MASTERPIECE.

THOU standest there, serene indeed a form
As e'eı Apollo conjured from the night
Or Dian sought again with silver rays.
There is not anything in all thyself
But telleth of the wisdom of the Gods
Who made thee like themselves, that thou shouldst
      take
Unblinded as thy right the seat beside
Olympian Zeus ; but now, thy friends being dead,
Lo, thou art left alone upon the earth
To dwell with pygmies in a world of pain.
Yea, ours thou art, but thine I will not be
To perish animate in thy marble arms.

DHU VORN.

SEE yonder river gliding through the plain
In silence to the immemorial sea,
Black as the clouds, instinct with memory,
She is all turned to tears which flow in vain,
Weeping they flow, for never drop can gain
That birch-tree glade, where glittering in glee
Ages agone they dwelt an hour with thee
And earned an immortality of pain.

     *   *   *   *   *

Oh for the rainbow art ! I knelt in prayer
Before the faintest shadowing of her
By one whose soul had slipped into his brush ;
Praying I knelt amid the inconscious rush
Of multitudes reëchoing, " woman ne'er
Was fair as this "—while I was kneeling there.

SYMBOLISM.

To sit and think, to lie and dream of thee
       Eternally
Till all the world's a symbol, as thy dress
The forest green, and as thy tenderness
       The snow-flake is.
Thyself thou art, but I am merged in thee ;
       No boat may be
More lost to earth, more thine eternally,
       That sinks at sea.

THE FURNACE.

HE hurled upon the flames a book of light,
Claspéd in gold, with rubies studded o'er ;
I gaze and shudder to the vision's core
Watching those many-coloured leaves invite
The forkèd fury of the conqueror ;—
One is all " Elfin," " Realized Delight"
Glows on a second ; on a third I saw
Rise the first sun for Adam from the night.
When all were burned a quivering shade remained,
Each colour mergèd in a ghostly gray,
Most eloquent of all their glories waned ;
Upsprung a breeze, and while they passed away
Methought a voice, as from the dead, did say —
" These are the ashes of a love disdained."

· THE VISION.

Last night I saw thee, not in dull disguise
Diurnal of base worldly intercourse,
But swimming in upon the tide of dreams
Thou dawnedst on me as in ancient days,
Imperial in imperial perfectness.
But wherefore didst thou whisper, as I thought,
" See where my hair is withered into gray " ?
I looked again, but lo, thine ivory brow
Shone out eternal from the radiant night—
And then again methought that such a ring
As once was ours had come upon my hand
All unbeknown, and turning round to seek
The riddle's meaning, read it in thine eyes
That fair brimmed o'er with heavenly promises.
Thus was my fate revoked—but lo, thy face
Sudden grows marble, and thy vanished eyes
Speak truth in silence from their scoopèd graves.

SPRINGTIDE.

OPEN the windows of thy soul
  And let the morning in,
Thy garden glows with the rathe primrose,
  The sweet spring days begin.
The dew still glitters in the cup
  So green the fairies love :
It is their wine, a draught divine,
  No tear from the sky above.

      *   *   *   *

Yet, yet beware the dove that sits
  Cooing upon the sill,
Her rosy beak of human blood
  Has not yet drunk its fill.

MEMORY

A. Let loose the locks of memory,
Let them stream along the wind,
And to the phantom of the past
The hideous present bind.
It may be she will reach thee yet
Alone in distant path,
The yellow ribbon in her hair
Gleams as an aftermath—
Then cease thy wail.
    B.   Had Death been kind,
As once her sister was,
No happier wight had taken flight—
    A. Thou blamest Death because
She did not strike when at thy hand
Ten thousand daggers stood.
Poltroon ! 'twas fear and her soft voice
That murmured "God is good."
    B. I could not tear myself away
From where myself was given ;

I could not seek for Paradise
When earth was hell and heaven ;
So grant me leave to play awhile,
Like idiots in the sun,
With gems, religion, power and art,
For life and death are one.

.

MUSIC.

WANDER along the grove while music plays,
Thine Ariadne be thy pensiveness,
Then will she lift thee into subtler sphere
Than any track of well-defined thought.
There fancy palpitates, the goal outstepped,
Like a white fawn when from her mother strayed
She lifts her eyes within a charmèd wood.

THE DEATH OF ARETINO.

PERSONS.

PIETRO ARETINO.
TIZIANO VECELLIO.
GIORGIONE.
ANTONIO MOROSINI (*A Gentleman of Venice*).
VERONICA FRANCO (*A Courtesan*).

SCENE.—VERONICA FRANCO'S *house in Venice.*

Aretino. The world has been asleep five hun-
    dred years,
Bound in the vellum of the Veronese ;
I drink her health renascent. (*He drinks.*)
    V. Franco. My fellow-townsman ! where does
    he abide ?
Loves he the revel ? Is he quick of wit,
Worthy divine Pietro ?
    Aretino. Give me a kiss, thou queen of inno-
    cents,
And yet another.   [*Tries to embrace her.*
    V. Franco.   Not the smallest touch
Thine of my lips shall know, till thou hast made
For such an insult due apology.

I

Titian. Well said, Veronica, and till he prove
His paradox, let Pietro drink alone.

V. Franco. (*Going to* TITIAN.) Are these the
   roses that should know my curls,
Or paler flowers, Vecellio ?

Titian.   Golden hair
Was never crowned as this ; ah for the day,
I'll make a Mary of thee shall eclipse
The best in Venice.

Aretino.   Titian, thou shalt watch
The daylight on her cheeks, for me the night
Paints her full lovelier—come, innocent !

       [*Approaches* VERONICA FRANCO.

V. Franco. No ! no ! Vecellio, keep me from
   the wretch ;
He'd rape the innocent.

Aretino.   Sweet ignorant !
Thine innocence is equal to a nun's.

Titian. See how he asks thy pardon.

V. Franco.   Now retract,
Pietro, thy naughty "ignorant."

Aretino.   Very well :
Ni te perdite amo ;—let me add
The kisses of the poem, bird as sweet
As ever fled from Lesbia.

      [*Takes* VERONICA FRANCO *from* TITIAN.

V. Franco. The Morosini comes to sup to-
night ;
Leave me some kisses for his amorous name.

Aretino. No, none, not any, neither smallest
touch
Of thy lips on to mine, but shall be stamped
Through with the signet of my love ; I dare
Antonio Morosini, were he Doge,
To mar one white page of my manuscript.

V. Franco. (*Embracing* ARETINO.) Ah ! Pietro, dear,
Thine am I.

Titian. (*Aside.*) And Venezia's.

Aretino.   Pass the wine :
Vesuvio bubbles in my veins to-night.

Titian. (*Going to the window.*) The star of
war is all afire to-night.

Aretino. (*To* GIORGIONE.) Make us some
melody, Giorgione,
Whereon our souls may float, like Mahomet's
corse,
Between the earth and heaven.

Giorgione. (*Taking his lute.*) What you will,
Divine Pietro, though a sleepless week,
Made up of love and labour, little lends
But discord to the music ; shall I play

The waving melody Soranzo loves ?
She says it sets her tapestry alive,
Veining the very stitches.

    V. Franco.   Pass the wine.
Here I baptize you.

       [*Pours a glass of red wine on* ARETINO'S
         head; it trickles down his face in thin
         streams.

    Aretino.   Evoë ! Evoë !

              [*Drinks.* GIORGIONE *plays.*

How sweet the music, like a wind that blew
Through Sappho's lyre, imprisoned till to-day
In Giorgione's lute.

    V. Franco.   Ah ! play again,
To please Veronica, Giorgione.

    Titian. (*From the window.*) I pray you, play
        again.

    Giorgione.   First, let us drink
The ruddiest hair that ever framed in red
The bluest eyes that ever moved the world.

                   [*They drink.*

    Aretino. I drink the eyes and hair, but you
        have left
The picture hardly drawn ; see now, I drink

                     [*He fills.*

The other veilèd marvels, little nose,

—That pinnacle of pride between the cheeks—
And those wet lips of her's, the goddess neck
Those breasts, white billows of a perfumed sea
Thighs, hips, and arms to rock the mariner
In weary joy asleep, I drink the rest   [*Drinks.*
In silence, deep as all its hidden bliss.
(*To* GIORGIONE.) I'll drink you drunk with
    jealousy !

  Giorgione.   Beware !
You are ablaze to-night, Pietro, none
As yet knows even her name, but you shall prove
Her every charm.

    V. Franco. (*Laughs.*) Ha ! ha ! none knows
      her name !
Save all the gondolieri and they know
More than Bianca's [1] face, where the very paint
Blushes for shame to cover such a skin.

    Giorgione.. 'Tis not Bianca.

    V. Franco.   Then another she,
An elder sister, were it possible.

    Aretino. (*Aside to* GIORGIONE.) Whisper her
      name.

    Giorgione. (*Going to* ARETINO.) Beware Ve-
      cellio !
Old Palma's daughter.

    [1] Bianca Capello, a famous courtesan of the period.

Aretino. (*Whispers.*) What, so soon untrue
To Titian?

Giorgione. (*Whispers.*) Yes, I met her at the
    mask;
Told her the lies that woman loves to hear;
The morrow came the message, "Titian's gone
To Malamocco; come and mourn his loss."

Aretino. Ha! ha! most excellent.

Titian. (*Coming from window.*) The moon's
    to-night
Curved like a sickle or Diana's horn.

Aretino. A horn, you said?

Titian.   A sickle or a horn,
Or what you will, Pietro.

Aretino.   Nay, a horn;
That is the happiest likeness, and methinks
Upon your brow yet dwells the lunar curve.

      [GIORGIONE *and* ARETINO *laugh loudly.*

V. Franco. Titian, Pietro and Giorgione
Keep whispering their secrets; let us make
Our mystery together.

Titian. (*Going to* VERONICA FRANCO.) Please
    comfort me,
I am alone to-night, Annina's ill;
These August suns, she says, have wearied
    her.

Giorgione. (*Whispers* ARETINO.) Then am I
   God Apollo !

Aretino. (*Laughing.*) Helios, hail !

Titian. (*Filling.*) Veronica ! a toast !

Aretino.   So, pass the wine.
Veronica, I drink you in this glass !
Come, melt the frown and let me drink it too.
Veronica ! Veronica !   [*They drink.*

  V. Franco. (*Smiling.*) Ah ! Pietro mine,
You'll coax his keys from Pietro.

  Giorgione. (*Rising.*)   I must go
Where Duty calls.

  Titian.   Thrice fortunate are you
To own so fair a Duty, prithee lay
Also my homage at the unknown shrine,
Curtained in russet, prankt with white and blue,
So like Annina. (*Sighs.*)

  Aretino. (*Laughing.*) Very like, indeed.

  V. Franco. (*Laughing.*) Old Palma's daughter !
   now the riddle 's clear,
'Twas not Bianca.

  Titian. (*Starting to his feet.*) By Madonna's
   soul,
Giorgione, you have not stolen my love ?

  Giorgione. No, Titian, never.

  Aretino. (*Laughing loudly.*) Nevermore than I

Who've known her well this twelve-month. .

   Giorgione.   By the stars,

Pietro, you lie !

   Aretino. (*Continues to laugh.*) Ha ! ha ! well
      then, I lie,

You lie, and Titian and the whole world lies

With the same lie.

     [*He falls face forward on the table and re-
      mains motionless. They all rush to him.
      *TITIAN *raises his head; it falls back.*

   Titian.   He 's dead.

   Giorgione.   Dead ?

Enter ANTONIO MOROSINI.

   Antonio.   Bona sera !

   V. Franco. (*Weeping.*) Antonio, Pietro's dead,
      divine Pietro !

   Antonio. Christ ! is Pietro dead?

   V. Franco. (*Taking* ANTONIO'S *hand and
      kissing it.*)   You'll stay to-night

And comfort me, Antonio ?

   Giorgione.   ⎫
   Titian.   ⎬   Pietro's dead !
           ⎭

     [*Exeunt* TITIAN *and* GIORGIONE.

THE END.

THE VISION.

I STOOD alone above the Leven lake
Amid the fairies' circle, where the trees
Draw back to watch their dance; the autumn
    breeze
Came tired to this old place, too tired to shake
One fir-tree cone, but ever as it passed
       Dead leaves kept falling fast

Within my heart, for I was very sad,
Thinking of Mary, Queen, and the blue spears
Glinting adown these shores in buried years.
Sudden beside me was a tiny lad,
His voice seemed faint, and, though he stood by
    me,
       Sounded beyond the sea.

" She is not gone," he said, "red hair and lip,
And many-changeful eyes, and the ruinous smile
Wreathing such sweet perdition in the isle
Yonder where once she dwelt, but as a ship

Full-sail a-tossing now upon thy brain
    I see the Queen again."

"Oh ancient man," I said (for now I saw
That he was very old), "I prithee tell
By what fell pact my secret soul you spell,
And who you are?" he answered, "By a law
Simple beyond thy ken, but who I be
    I will reveal to thee:

"Merlin I was in England yesterage,
Silviano for infant Italy,
The better part of Faust; here I am he
That wrought King Fairy bale and mickle rage
Kissing his Queen by magic of the moon,—
    Thomas of Ercildoune.

"And (for thou couldst not see me otherwise,
And only here mid-circle of the ring,)
Thou art of ours, no vain imagining
Which as thou thinkst deep in thy being lies
But is for me clear, clearer than the sphere
    Of yonder placid mere."

He pointed to the lake that then was glowing
Beneath a coloured cloud; I did discern
Rise to the sky-line from the little burn

Two purple herns, and though I watched their
      going,
Anxious, intent, no way they seemed to gain,
            Circling around in vain.

"They are enchantèd birds," he said, "at eve
They rise and circle till the twilight dies ;
'Twas Mary charmed them, and her island lies
Midway their circular flight, for her they grieve
Hopeless as thou ; deep doting on their grief
            They would disdain relief,

"And if perchance the tide of ages rolled
Back on its waves, and the belovèd Queen
Reignèd secure in royalty serene,
Thou and these birds would seek some other-
      where
            A queen for their despair.

"Wide is the dæmon circle, and you ride
Æons apart the centre where I stand
Heart to the mystery's heart, but there is a band
Woven of lights, thoughts, scents and sounds,
      that hide
Their secret from the uniniate—
            These link our fate.

"Such are our gems and flower, the chrysophras,
The opal with her green and milky lights,
Mimosa asking love from those who pass
Then dying when the kiss upon her lights,
Such also that sweet singing of the swan
   Unheard yet dreamed upon.

"And all these things are phases of the vision,
Changing from age to age its symbolry,
Whereof we are part, fast fixed beyond division
To the sad secret of our destiny."
He paused, I heard the tinkling of her bells
  Whereof his legend tells.

"Thomas," I said, "bide yet with me awhile,
Fain in this charmed roundel would I see
The regent-soul to do her fealty."
Then fathom-sunk rose to his lips a smile,
Like murderous pearl unclenched from diver's
   hand
   Who brings it dead to land.

"Oh temerous moth that vagrantly awinging
Followest the light that dances on the moss
Hither and thither fluttering till across

Some reed-bound pool the moon her image
    flinging
Drowns 'i the rippling circle of her mirth,
    Such thy request is worth.

" But for the sake of the dæmonic spark
That doth inform thy clay, I will reveal
What most of things dæmonic thou mayest feel
And perish not ; look in my eyes and mark
What with thine eyes thou mayest on earth be-
    hold
        Multiplied millionfold."

Then suddenly I felt as though, expanding,
Earth's total store of joy myself contained,
Round me, as on a mountain crest, were standing
A thousand perfect forms, and each retained
The crown as of a thousand wars victorious,
Placed on their brows by my transcendant
    power ;
A light as of the seventh heaven shone o'er us,
Bliss-plumed I soared on the triumphal hour.
Sudden, I felt as though a chasm were riven
Deep in my central self wherein they fell,
And like a vapour from the chasm arisen,
Anguish ecstatic folded me in hell.

Then I beheld their thousand hands a-waving
Farewell eternal through the hopeless night,
Felt wafted kisses in my piercèd craving,
Each one the last upon my lips alight.

    *   *   *   *   *

    *   *   *   *   *

    *   *   *   *   *

When I awoke the day had come again,
Thomas was gone with all his wizardry,
And I alone, save for a crested wren
Who in his beak a leaf of chestnut-tree
Had brought to wreathe the corse, and stood
    amazed
        Seeing the dead man raised.

HYMN.

"Le not your hearts be troubled ; ye believe in God, believe also in me."—*John*, xiv. 1.

"LET not your hearts be troubled," were
  The soft last words He laid
For ointment on His soldiers' wounds,
  "Children be not dismayed."
"I go but to prepare a place
  For those that follow me,
I come again to bid you all
  Welcome eternally.
Let not your minds be troubled with
  Celestial symbolry,
The youngest cherub in God's house
  Knoweth the Trinity.
Ye that believe in God, believe,
  Love and believe in me,
His only son, I saw Him weave
  In Heaven Earth's mystery."

THE SPHINX.

I HAVE touched the heart of the world, and know
    The abyss of woe :
Nothing can wring from me sorrow or joy,
    No earthy alloy
Troubles the soul, informs the mind that probes
    The fiery globes.
I am all the world to myself ; I am burning hell,
    I am heaven as well.
Mine eyelid's fringe moves never an inch to
    behold
    The plague unfold
Her leopardine mantle and motherwise gather
    Mortals together.
My atoms are essence you shiver in vain,
    They form again.
The world is a thought that proceeds from my
    head,
    I am living and dead.

AFTER READING MAETERLINCK'S "AVEUGLES."

THROW off the veil, here is no palace hall
For golden epithet and glittering rhyme,
Here words are steel and stone—transpierce or
      fall
By natural law—here where the only crime
Is to be blind, to have never seen the sun
Sail through his realm at midday, to have known
Midnight a hundred years (and there was one
Far older sat among them).   Life is sown
So deep with sorrow that at length may rise,
Piled on the grief of ages, to the skies
Some word supreme, some vision fit to tell
The gods they slumber mingling earth and hell
—Vision and word ;—*on dit que tu es belle*,
And poor blind hands seeking the asphodel.

K

SARAH BERNHARDT AS THEODORA
ENTHRONED.

WHAT further incense can my trembling plume
Waft with those clouds that are your heraldry?—
The Orient lightens in your pearls, and by
The tiger couchant 'neath the lily's bloom
You sceptre love and symbolize the doom
That blinded him who dared, with bleary eye,
Gaze where above, in height of empery,
Throned the last scion of Slavonian groom.

Said I "the last" and read the legend right,
You and not you, a soul within a soul,
Where many souls take refuge from the night,
And speechful through thy lips again unroll
Of their great deeds the reëmblazoned scroll,
Sarah Lucifera, the queen of light?

WITH A COPY OF KEATS.

THOU that wast once to me
More than all gods may be,
Than respite from the strife
Of most disastrous life,
Take back this holy book
But never dare to look,
Traitress to love and art,
Into Endymion's heart,
Lest there thy soul discern,
Shrined in the Grecian urn,
Veiled in Corinthian eyes,
Lamia's paradise
Mirrored in Saturn's face,
Murdered of all its grace,
Despair, dead Hope's dear child.

BLUE-RAVEN locks and under
  In those her deep eyes, lay
The secret of all colours
  That turn the night to day ;

For they were full of sunsets,
  Blue-heaving morning sea,
Of tiger's topaz gazing,
  Of all the joys that be.

And all these things for ever,
  For ever never thine—
Go burn thy soul to ashes
  And wallow with the swine.

"LET down your hair, sweet Sibyl," was my
    prayer,
       "Your glorious hair
This only once ; we are alone, but were
      Olympus there,
      What god so fair?"—
She smiled and looked, and smiled and laughing
    drew
      A gold pin through
Their coiled brown, then suddenly there flew
      Such-wise as do
      The brave bright blue
Sea waves that love their lady, roll on roll,
      And hid the whole
Of her fair form, hid time, and hold my soul
      In their control
      While ages roll.

"How wisely the heroes of Greece
    Are buried away!
Poor creatures, they sleep now in peace
    From jealousy!"
"How sweetly my poet can talk"
    (She smiled as we kissed),
"Our genius and beauty shall walk .
    Crowned as they list."
So sounds her soft voice in my ear
    Like a tinkling bell,
But the chime that for marriage rings clear
    Tolls forth the knell—
And I whom my fate outran
    Now lying alone,
I know I was only a man
    And she a stone.

LOVE (A CONCEIT).

SPEAK to me not of love, it is a word
Cosmic, coëval with the mysteries
That barrier off our being, never heard
Without the echo Life, and Him that is
Father and Son of both, mysterious Death.
Call Love the diamond myriad-faceted
That pins the ostrich plume, or chokes[1] his
     breath
Who dared engulf the eye of idolhead.
Or (for our humour runs to metaphor)
He is the cloud that on an April day
Smiles sunny tears upon the labourer
And almost touches earth, then floats away
Far in the blue to robe the fading skies
In rosy crape to greet his closing eyes.

[1] There is a story to the effect that the diamond eye
of an idol was picked out and swallowed by a thief.

INTERJECTIONS.

I LOVED you far too well
    Ever to tell
How much I loved you more than well.

FATHOMS deep in the past !
I stand and gaze aghast
Down fathoms of the past.

TO THE STARS.
YE golden corpses buried in the air.

THE deep red rose eternal of my love.

THOU canst not give me heaven, then give me
    hell.

TO THÉOPHILE GAUTIER.

O RAINBOW soul that overspanned a sky
Black with creed mist exhaled in Galilee.

TO ALBIUS TIBULLUS.

SWEET poet, I have held thy hand
   Across the stream of years,
Ours the same soul, same time and land,
   Same love, same hopes and fears.

A POETIC CREED REVERSED.

(BYRON, *Don Juan*, Canto I., ccv.)

THOU shalt believe in Shelley, Swinburne, Keats.
  Thou shalt not set up Dryden, Pope, or Byron;
The first is stiff, stuffed full of quaint conceits,
  The second prose, the third thou soon must
    tire on,
Despite long series of athletic feats—
  Metre and rhyme beat flat as with an iron—
And own Keats' soul indeed a "fiery particle"
Snuffed out by neither Byron nor "an article."

POSTSCRIPT.

As one that seeking aureate grain
Youthlong has delved the burning plain,
Now sick at heart, now sudden bold,
Swearing he does, does not behold
Mixed with the siftings of the pan
One "colour"[1] speck of gold,
Sudden arising, grown to man,
Hurls all upon the river,
And presses on with emptied hands
Toward untrodden glittering sands,
Toward Herodotean lands,
Blue vistas opening ever,—
So I this book, nor turn to see
The whelming swirl nor the wind's fury ;
This no more is a part of me
Who press toward the untrodden strands,
Toward Herodotean lands,
Blue vistas opening ever.

[1] "Colour" gold. The grains of gold found by the
digger who is prospecting are thus called.

www.ingramcontent.com/pod-product-compliance
Lightning Source LLC
Chambersburg PA
CBHW031121020726
47495CB00007B/2297